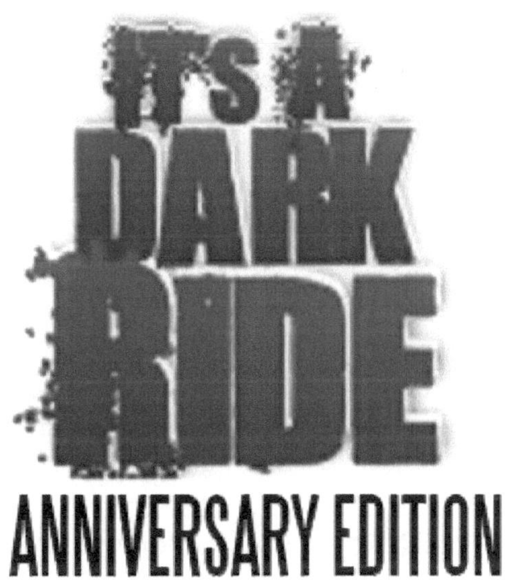

David K. Montoya

www.darkmythpublications.com

Dark Myth Publications
145 S Glenoaks Blvd.
Unit #3149,
Burbank, CA 91502

ISBN: 979-8-9906083-2-0
First Printing August 2024

Dark Myth Publications is a registered trademark of The JayZoMon Dark Myth Company, LLC.

10 9 8 7 6 5 4 3 2 1

Books by David K. Montoya:

- **Alis** – Dark Myth Publications – 2023
- **Through the Eyes of Madness** – Dark Myth Publications – 2023
- **The Missing Unicorn in the Land of the Zombie Fairies** – M–Kids Press – 2020
- **It's A Dark Ride** – Dark Myth Publications – 2014

Other works by David K. Montoya:

- **The Monster Within: Tales of a Tortured Mind**
  – *Andy* – Zombie Works Publications – 2023
- **Unwelcomed Stories of Hauntings and Possessions** – *Can You Hear Me Now* – 2022
- **The World of Myth Anthology Vol.4** – *Day of the Easter Bunny* – Dark Myth Publications – 2021
- **Who's Who of Emerging Writers 2021** – *Introduction* – Sweetycat Press – 2021
- **Full Moon & Howlin: A Werewolf Anthology** – *Elizabeth* – Zombie Works Publications – 2020
- **I, The Writer** – *Thoughts* – Sweetycat Press – 2020
- **Monsterthology 2** – *Black Lagoon* – Zombie Works Publications – 2019

Other works by David K. Montoya: (Con't)

- **The Black Widow Paperback** – *Chapter Five* – The International Writers Of Justice – 2019
- **The World of Myth Anthology Vol.3** – *The Leftovers* – Dark Myth Publications – 2018
- **Zombie EPICdemic** – *Dead Space* – Zombie Works Publications – 2018
- **The World of Myth Anthology Vol.2** – *Riding Shotgun* – Dark Myth Publications – 2010

The World of Myth Anthology Vol.1 – *Foresight/Sleepy Hollow* – Dark Myth Publications – 2007

DEDICATED

I want to dedicate this anniversary edition to all that has passed since I wrote the book. I feel lucky and unworthy to be here still and you are not.

Randolph C. Lofgren, Lacie Montoya, Stephanie Zuniga, Joshua Henderson, Terry D. Scheerer, William V. Dewbre Jr., Virgil and Anita Dewbre, Stanley M. Lieber, Shawn Morton, Millie and Bob Harger, Gerald Duncan, and David Zuniga Sr.

The world is a sadder, darker place without these people.

Table of Contents

INTRODUCTION

Welcome back, and for those who his the first trip in 2014 be welcome to this anniversary edition of It's A Dark Ride. To prepare for this event, I re-read my original introduction as I spoke about moving from writing comic books to short stories and how I did not call my stuff horror and proclaimed it was dark fiction. I mentioned my mentor, and then rambled on about authors who are famous and how they wrote what they knew. Then somehow got into my religious upbringing and how I was wrapped up as a small adolescent and working in an ICU made things worse in my crafting *dark* stories.

One thing I would like to do is take the time to tell my past self--SHUT THE HELL UP! No one cares!

Second, I would tell him that while *write what you know* is a solid number two on the rules of being a writer, he neglected to mention the first commandment which is *write for yourself.* My past self failed to talk about *why* these stories were created and why it took two years after you finished to publish the book. How you were tired and unhappy with life, but after you lost your position at the hospital for someone younger, cheaper and, I only assume at this next one, not as much as an asshole Evil Dave was. If you know you know...that or if I ever gather the courage to write an autobiography.

My unhappiness was exacerbated into depression after I lost my house, my truck, my friends, and my way of living and found myself, my wife, and my autistic son in a Uhaul on the way to Northern Nevada. While I was there I began to dream about suicide and wanted to make my exit from this world. I started waking up in the dead of night and I just pondered life, eventually just sliding back into bed and falling back to sleep. In one of these late-night episodes, I woke up and wandered behind a keyboard and surfed the web, I grew bored of it and caught myself looking at old publication files on the desktop. I clicked on a folder that was named *itsadarkride* I remembered starting this in 2009 or 2010 writing Sweet Dreams Are Made of This, The Gift, and Lola's Special Gift for the publication. I opened it to find eight stories the three I just mentioned and five I selected many years ago for an anthology of my short stories. It was at that moment I decided that I would write seven new tales and *finally* make my own book.

I ended up writing five stories, Can You Hear Me Now, The Last Supper, Call of the Black Bird, Dead Heat and It's A Dark Ride, although I ended up replacing Dead Heat with The Left Overs right before it went to editing. I created this book as an ode to my mentor Terry D. Scheerer's publication which inspired me to go into short stories, *Dreams of Darkness, Dreams of Night,* but the anger, the hate, the loathing, the desperation, the hopelessness and the evil were all dedications to each personal demon I fought at the time.

And, finally, the final thing I would like to pass on to my younger self is that was the preparation for what was to come.

You thought you were *alone* in 2010 and 2011?

As I sit here, I am sorry to report that most of everyone you love has passed away. Randy was the first in 2011, Lacie too, and then Terry died a few months later. Virgil is gone, and Shawn is even gone. There are more that could be mentioned, but I do not have the self-will to continue.

But, I will say to my Past Self that it does get better. During that time you have also brought two amazing daughters into the world, Jay has graduated and is healthy and happy. You have found new friends who have become non-food relatives, restored old friendships, and even found love again. I know that *It's a dark ride and no one makes it out alive.*

Yet as a decade has passed, I need to make an addendum to that and say that, yes, *It's a dark ride and no one makes it out alive. But that does not mean you shouldn't make the best of your one shot at it.*

Until we meet again, perhaps in another ten years!

With love and respect to all,

David K. Montoya
Apple Valley, CA
April 5, 2024

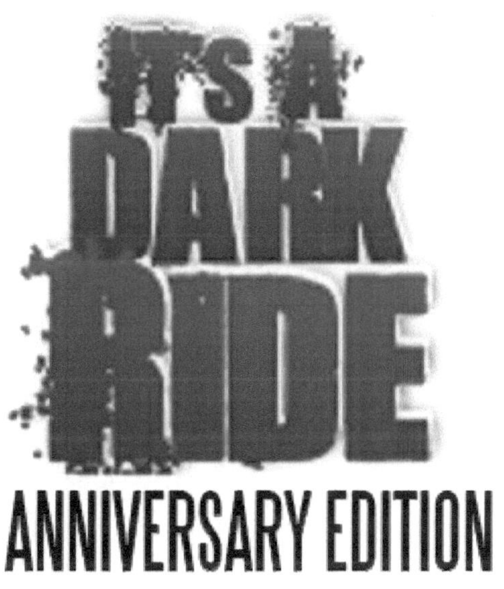
IT'S A
DARK
RIDE
ANNIVERSARY EDITION

SWEET DREAMS ARE MADE OF THIS

A LIGHT DEW gently covered the graveyard by the time I arrived. I had tried to put this off for as long as I could, but I am here before the night's end a from the day she was taken from me.

I found her headstone in the far east corner of the cemetery. It was the first time I saw the granite marker; I couldn't bear the thought of her in that casket – so I didn't go. But I was here for her now, and that had to count for something.

I knelt tearing the overgrown grass away from the tombstone until I saw her name.

Bella Badkin
1982-2014
Missed here on Earth but welcomed at the gates of Heaven.

"My dear Bella," I murmured to myself. God only knew just how much I missed her. I would have done anything to have her back in my arms, even if it were only for one night. My vision obscured as the tears flowed down my face. Trying my best not to allow my mind to recreate the past, but unable to resist.

#

I clearly remember the last night I saw her alive. It was September, at a time we had horrible weather where we lived. Bella and I were in insurance sales, and specialized in automobiles policies. We were quite busy with all the bad weather.

Sometimes, I would lose myself watching her work. To me, it was watching poetry in motion. She was smart and beautiful, but the best part was that she was MY girl. We were happy together. There was nothing better than knowing such beautiful creature was going to be beside me when I woke up in the morning.

That night, I had finished with my claims before Bella. Waiting for her over an hour. It was around ten o'clock when I felt a gentle snug. Looking up heavy-eyed saw her smiling down at me.

"Why don't you run along home, sweetie? I'm gonna be here for a few more hours," Bella's voice was warm and soft.

I pulled my thoughts together before I answering. "You know you are amazing, Bella?"

Her smile grew wider. She was not one for praise. Bella wrapped her arms around me and placed a soft kiss upon my lips. "Oh, Vernon, you are the sweetest as always!"

I would have held her forever if I had known that that would be our last kiss. We stood there for several moments without anything said. Words were not important at that moment. At that very second in time, nothing was more important to me than the warmth of her body. If only I had known, I'd never have left her.

"Alright, Bells, what time can I expect ya home?" I asked her while I continued to hold onto her tightly.

"I should be done in hour and a half," Bella said. I saw the exhaustion in her eyes. I wanted her to leave everything until the following morning, but I knew it was pointless if I attempted to persuade her otherwise.

"Then, I will see you at 11:30?"

"Until then, Lover," Bella softly said. She gave me one last kiss before I walked out of the office. Outside, the rain poured so hard I could barely see my hand in front of my face. The atmosphere was quite different from a typical September night; it was hot and humid. The air stuck to my lungs as I breathed in. I thought something was wrong, but no clue how correct that thought would become.

#

At 11:30 pm on the nose Bella walked out of the office. The rain continued to fall, but now a thick fog had settled in, making visibility impossible.

According to the surveillance video, Bella pulled out of the driveway five minutes after she walked out of the office building. It appeared that the rain let up some, but the fog was so dense it would have been like driving blindfolded for fifteen miles, which meant she drove the car at a plodding speed.

The police were surprised that she made it as far as she did, and the coroner estimated that it was five minutes after midnight when Bella drove her car off the side embankment. The vehicle plummeted forty feet when it crashed into the woods below. Bella was ejected through the windshield even though she wore her seat belt; it snapped upon impact.

#

That was a year ago today. If only I had... If I had done something different. She would still be alive today. All I have left is my memories of her: her smile, laughter, and beauty. Standing at her gravesite for a few more moments I could no longer bear to be there.

I placed her favorite flowers by the headstone, feeling small raindrops on the back of my neck. By the time I reached the cast-iron gate, the rain was pouring, making it gloomy and cold – but for the moment, it was quite befitting.

#

Five minutes after midnight I opened my eyes and lay there for a moment before I felt a warm breath on the back of my neck. Confusion set in as I sat up in my bed, then I saw her. Bella was snuggled next to me and appeared to be perfectly at peace.

I watched her as she opened her eyes and broke a smile. *I must be dreaming again, huh?*

"It is what it is, Love," Bella said as if she read my thoughts. I threw my arms around her. It did not make sense happened at that moment. But I was allowed to be with her once more, and to me, that was all that mattered. I held her for some time before she pushed me softly away.

"W-where are you going?" I asked as she got out of bed. Bella paused for a moment and looked over my way with an amused smile.

"Don't worry, Vernon, I'm not leaving you again."

My heart fluttered with those words. Could it be possible that a higher power allowed my love to return to me? It didn't matter, nor did I care as long as I had her in my arms once again. I swore to myself that this time I would not let anything happen to her; *Not this time!*

"Oh, I want to show you something special, but you're gonna have to close your eyes," Bella said with a flirtatious smile. "And you can't open them until I tell you to, okay Lover?"

"Okay," I said, "I hope it's good."

"Oh, trust me!" Bella said. I felt her hand as it traveled up my leg. "Go ahead and open your eyes, Lover."

What happened next was not what I expected when I opened my eyes. I saw a thing that only resembled Bella. In a panic, I jumped back, my head slammed into the wooden headboard of my bed. The creature slowly moved back onto the bed as it crawled toward me. I saw the abomination in the moonlight. It was Bella, but it was not the beautiful woman I once knew. Her skin was dried and hard, and as she moved bits of flesh fell from her. Her once luxurious hair appeared to have fallen out, except for a few strands. The bone of her skull was more visible than the small remnants of skin that remained patched together covering her face.

I screamed the first thing that came to my mind, "What the Hell?" The rotting creature crawled only inches from my face as she spoke. I couldn't help but gag – the smell was indescribable. It could be compared to a sitting septic tank opened for the first time in years.

“This is to die for, Lover,” Bella hissed.

I did the only thing I could do – I screamed for my life, but even that did no good.

The End

THE GIFT

MICHAEAL RINSTROM ALWAYS wanted to be a famous entertainer. For most of his life, he wanted to see himself on a grand stage in front of thousands of fans who would be screaming his name. As a child, he had imagined that he would be a living legend by the age of twenty.

Now, at the age of thirty-three, he worked at a local Piggly Wiggly store as a clerk. While he had not managed to reach his goal being a famous star at an early age, he never gave up his dream - of being like his idol, Sir Elton John. In an effort to keep his dreams alive, whenever possible, Michael would make his rounds to local theaters, entering tryouts for musicals and going to any singing audition announced. While he could tell that people liked his musical ability, he never seemed to make that final cut. Deep down inside he knew, that his singing voice was good, but he apparently lacked that special "magic touch" that would make him sound great.

One day, he heard that Scott Ireson, a well-known Elton John impersonator, was booked to host a charity concert in Micheal's hometown. Ireson, who usually performed on the main stages of Las Vegas, needed an act to open for him during the charity show, and he wanted it to be a local personality. It was the break that Rinstrom had been waiting for, and knew this might be his last chance to get out of there and prove himself worthy to be in the spotlight finally and really shine. Michael also knew that he would have to do something impressive to woo the show producers, but what could he do this time, which he had never been able to accomplish during his other auditions?

#

In the theater before his audition, Michael was a nervous wreck. Backstage, he paced first one way then the other, frequently wiping his sweaty palms against his pants.

He usually wasn't so nervous before an audition, but Rinstrom somehow felt that this was the last chance he was ever going to have to make his life-long dream come true, and if he failed, he would never get another such opportunity. That thought was ridiculous, he knew, but the premonition, if that was what it was, would not go away. He tried to focus on the song that he would sing, but the unusual apprehension that surrounded him still lingered.

When it was time for his audition, a young man showed him to his marker on the stage. Michael squinted through the lights and could just see three people, two men and a woman, seated in the otherwise empty theater about six rows back. He stood there, waiting nervously, as the spectators whispered together and shuffled through papers. The added wait time was agony for Michael.

Finally, one of the people in the audience looked up at him and spoke. "Mr. Rinstrom, I'm Carl, one of the producers of this show. Thank you for coming today. What would you like to sing for us?"

Michael swallowed hard and had trouble finding his voice. "Um, it will be 'Candle in the Wind,' sir."

"Fine. The stage is yours, Mr. Rinstrom.

He took a deep breath and realized that he might not be able to do this after all. The nervousness that he had felt earlier seemed to have progressed to a tangible fear, and he found himself frozen in place. Nearing panic, he looked beyond the expectant producers to the enormous empty theater, where thick shadows draped the interior, and darkness protected the fading gilt of the aged decorations from prying eyes. At the back of the theater, over one of the doors, a red "Exit" sign glowed faintly in the gloom. That's what Michael wanted now - an exit, a way out of this hellish nightmare he had managed to get himself in.

He kept his gaze locked on that 'Exit" sign – at least it was something tangible, something real – and tried to find his voice, tried to salvage something of this fiasco. It was no use. His throat had locked up, and he knew that if he opened his mouth, nothing more than a sad and pathetic squeak would come forth.

He was about to call it quits and walk off stage at that moment and give up on his dream, when something caught his eye at the rear of the theater. A blob of darkness, blacker than the surrounding gloom, that detached itself from the shadows and moved slowly into a position just beneath the glowing 'Exit' sign. Rinstrom stared at the undulating apparition feeling an unexpected sensation flow over him, almost as if the fright and panic that had paralyzed him was washed away. The sign over the exit, which moments before had been a mere glow in the darkened theater, now began to brighten and pulse until it shone a bright and fiery red, and the letters seemed three times their average size. *Now that's an exit sign*. Oddly enough, he had wished for a way out, for a 'sign' that things were going to be somehow all right, and now he felt what he wanted had been unveiled.

A feeling of power and boldness came over Michael, replacing the fear that had held him so tightly confined. Slowly, he closed his eyes and began to sing without even thinking. For the first time in his life, he felt the music swell within him, and he projected his vocal cords to a perfect pitch. The song's words flowed from him like fresh snow-melt cascading over new falls - pure, clear, and sharp. Michael was elated, and free. Those feelings translated into his song.

After the flawless execution of an extended version of ' Candle in the Wind,' he stood there in silence, with his eyes still closed, absorbing the feel of what had just happened to him. It was several moments before he realized the faint 'clacking' sound he heard was actual applause. He opened his eyes to see the three producers standing in front of their seats, clapping their hands together for *him*.

"That was wonderful," the woman said, as the smiling men nodded in agreement.

"Um, thanks. Thank you very much," Michael replied shyly. "Uh, so... do I get the spot?"

One of the producers moved from where they had been standing and started down the aisle toward the stage. The guy was smiling up at Michael, but he could tell something was still wrong.

"I'm Carl, and the song was great," He mounted the stage and came up beside Rinstrom. "You sounded so much like the real thing – but, well, you just stood there, dude, like a bump on a log," he explained sadly. "I'm sorry, Mr. Rinstrom, but this is going to be a live show, and after all, the purpose of an opening act is to fire up the crowd and get them excited for the opening act."

"What my colleague is trying to say," the female producer said as she too walked up to Michael, "is that even though you sound fantastic, you just aren't what we're looking for in an opening act."

"My being frozen like that was just because of a little stage fright," Michael tried to explain, thinking fast. He couldn't let this slip away from him. Not now – not after what he had experienced. "I've been waiting for this opportunity my whole life. I know I can put on the kind of performance you are expecting. Please, is there anything I can do to make you change your minds?" he asked, looking from one face to the other.

"Hang on just a sec," Carl said, as he and his companion moved back to confer with the third producer. After a few moments, their discussion ended, and Carl turned around to the stage.

"Okay, here's the deal. There was only one other tryout who came anywhere near to matching your vocal talent. The guy doesn't have your range or your passion, but he put on a hell of a show, and that's something we have to consider in an opening act. You understand that, don't you?" Michael nodded, his heart sinking.

"But," Carl went on, "if for some reason, this guy can't perform tomorrow night, then the gig is definitely yours. Fair enough?"

"Yes, sir. That's great, really," he replied, his hopes rising once more.

"Now, don't get your hopes up too high," Carl said as if reading Michael's thoughts. "We're pretty sure he won't change his mind, so other than him dropping off the face of the Earth or something, it doesn't look like this is going to happen for you. At least not tomorrow," he added, giving Rinstrom something else to hang on to. "All right?"

"Okay," Michael said, nodding and smiling. "Thank you. Thank you *very* much," then left the stage and headed out of the theater.

#

Michael had taken a bus over to the audition, but when he got outside the theater, it was such a beautiful day, and he was still feeling so elated from his performance that he decided to walk home. He was a few blocks from the theater when he remembered a shortcut that he could take, which might cut as much as thirty minutes off his homeward trek.

Ordinarily, he wouldn't have considered using this shortcut since it involved having to traverse a long, dark, especially creepy alleyway that held bad memories for him. Memories that went back to his childhood, and he would rather not have to face them again. But, now, he felt that he could deal with anything. He felt strong, stronger than he could ever remember feeling, and the dark alley held no such fear for him today.

When he turned off the street, he was still reliving his incredible audition, and the alley didn't appear nearly as dark and menacing as he remembered from childhood. He continued walking for about fifteen minutes before wondering how long this alley truly was. He hadn't been paying much attention to his surroundings for quite some time, so wrapped up in his exciting afternoon.

Now Michael noticed that the tops of the buildings on either side of him seemed to lean in toward each other, blocking out the light making the alley appear very narrow and dark. He turned to look behind himself, and the entrance to the path seemed small and far away, resembling a point of light at the end of a long, dark tunnel. Michael hurried through the alley, feeling somewhat anxious, wanting very much to reach the end.

Nearing the end of the alley, Michael was running, as he was eager to get himself out of that dark tunnel. He burst into the welcome light, panting from his exertions. Stopped and leaned against a nearby hitching post for a few moments to catch his breath and settle his frayed nerves.

When he felt better, Michael straightened and turned back to look at what he had leaned on. A hitching post? What was a hitching post doing here? Michael stood on the edge of a road covered in dirt instead of one paved with asphalt noticing that it was extremely quiet. There was no sound of traffic (either cars or horses), nor bird or insect sounds. Where were all the people? More curious than frightened, Michael looked around surprised to see that the part of town he found himself in was utterly alien to what was supposed to be there. The building architecture was out of place for the current century and possibly for the entire planet.

Michael moved into the middle of the road to get a better view of each side of the street. Some of the buildings looked to be wood, perhaps after the style of the late 1800's—at least those dwellings were somewhat familiar, but nowhere did he see any sign of electricity. There were no neon signs in evidence, no streetlamps, and no signal lights. The rest of the buildings along the street were assorted styles, built with various materials, some familiar and some utterly bizarre. As he walked down the road, he passed buildings made of brick or stone, resembling boulders with doors and windows punched into the rock in odd places, as well as long, low buildings made of metal. Farther down there were huts built of thatch, with roofs of opaque plastic.

The whole place was too weird for Michael – he felt transported into another dimension or something equally bizarre and wanted to get out of there and go back home. The silence and number of unusual buildings were beginning to get on his nerves. He continued heading west in the direction he should have been going to reach his apartment becoming increasingly uneasy as he watched the sun sinking toward the horizon. He certainly didn't want to be caught in this 'town' after the sun disappeared.

Walking another block down the unusual street the prolonged silence he endured broke with a voice calling out to him. "Howdy, pardner. Not from around these parts, are ya?"

Michael so startled by hearing someone speak that he lost his balance and stumbled, having to catch his balance before slowly turning around to see who had addressed him. He did not know what to expect from the mystery speaker but or whoever, was related to the 'weird' section of this town. Then, from the shadow of a nearby building, a figure stepped into the light, and Michael sighed with relief to see that it was indeed a man walking toward him.

The stranger was tall and thin, dressed in a black, old-fashioned suit, including a black shirt, together with a tall-crowned, wide-brimmed hat. He offered a friendly smile as he advanced, so Michael said, "Uh, hello." He wasn't sure about this guy, since he could possibly be a resident of this place and all, but he wanted to keep an open mind.

"Didn't mean to startle ya, son," the man said as he came up to Michael. His voice was pleasant and gentle, calming Michael's apprehension. "Don't get many visitors, hereabouts," said the stranger.

"Oh, that's all right," he said, then turned and continued walking. The man kept pace with him, so Michael said, "I believe you don't get many visitors. Sorry, but this place gives me the creeps."

"Really?" the man said, gazing around at the oddly shaped buildings. "I find it very peaceful and relaxing, actually."

Michael smiled,he was beginning to like this guy. "Well, everybody has their own taste, I suppose."

"That's what found. The name's Luci, by the way."

"Lucy?" Michael asked. That seemed a bit odd, but then this whole place was more than a bit weird.

"No, it's Luci, with an "i"at the end," seeming to read Michael's thoughts. "It's just a nickname, but I'm used to it."

"Oh. Well, hi. I'm Michael Rinstrom," he told the man, and since they were still walking, he didn't bother offering his hand.

"Say, I know you," Luci said, snapping his fingers. "You're the fella what got screwed over at the audition today, right?"

"Well, I don't know that I got 'screwed,' but yeah, I

was at the audition today," Michael wondered how this stranger knew about what had happened to him.

"Ah, you were so much better than the other guy. It should be you up on that stage tomorrow night, singing your heart out, you know?"

"Uh, thanks. Believe me, I would give anything to sing at that concert tomorrow, but we don't always get what we want," Michael admitted with a shrug of his shoulders.

"Sure, you do," Luci said softly.

"Huh? I'm sorry, what did you say?" Michael asked, not sure that he had heard the man correctly.

"I said, sure, you can get whatever you want out of life if you have the right connections, that is."

"Oh. Well, obviously I don't have the right connections, then," Michael told him with a slight smile.

"Maybe you do, son. Maybe you do," Luci said, returning the smile.

Michael stopped and turned to face the older man. "Look, um, Luci. I don't understand what you're talking about, but I'm very serious about my singing."

"I know you are, son," Luci said softly and put his hand on Michael's shoulder. Startled at first by Luci taking the liberty of touching him, Michael relaxed after looking into the man's eyes and seeing only genuine concern. "That's why I want to help you," he added, gently squeezing the shoulder, then dropping his hand. "Let me show you something."

"Uh," Michael said, glancing toward the sun and noting that it would be dark in less than an hour.

"Don't worry about it, son," Luci said, again reading Michael's thoughts. "This will only take a few minutes, and I'll make sure you get home afterward." Since he still looked uncertain, Luci added, "It'll be worth your while, son. Believe me."

Michael didn't know why, but he suddenly felt as if he could trust this man, so he said, "All right. What have I got to lose?"

Luci offered him a wide smile in answer to that question and said, "C'mon, then, it's just a couple of doors down."

"What is?" Michael asked, following Luci up a set of wooden steps, and stopping in front of an antique (or junk) store. It was dark inside, the windows were dusty, but Michael could see rows of shelves lining the walls, along with a number of tables and counters, all of them covered with objects he couldn't identify from outside. Luci pulled a large ring of keys from his coat pocket and unlocked one of the double doors.

"Welcome to my own little slice of... heaven," Luci said, throwing open the door so Michael could enter.

He stepped inside and looked around. The sun was quickly sinking and very little light found its way past the dirty windows. Michael was unable to see too much, other than row after row of tables and ceiling-high shelves stretching back into the dim recesses of the store. The door closed behind him, when he heard a match strike and Luci lit an old fashioned kerosene lamp.

The glow from the lamp gave a small circle of light that brightened the immediate area around them.

Michael could see some items near him on the tables and shelves, amazed at what he saw. All manner of personal belongings, from expensive jewelry to worthless trinkets such as gloves, pairs of glasses, rings, a letter opener, an old camera, empty picture frames, necklaces, a pair of socks; he couldn't even imagine what else was present. On the shelves were stacks and stacks of books and a variety of boxes – some of them were music boxes, jewelry boxes, shoe boxes, small file boxes, pillboxes, hat boxes – the list went on.

As he moved farther into the 'store,' he saw knives, daggers, and swords piled up on the shelves along with pistols of all makes and calibers, together with boxes of ammunition and loose cartridges just lying around. The tables carried all manner of jetsam; watches, rings, cuff links, necklaces, bracelets – some of the items looked like they contained real gems; diamonds, rubies, pearls, sapphires. Michael was amazed but confused by the extravagant display. He turned to the strange man and asked, "What is all of this?"

Luci smiled and looked lovingly around at his treasures. "This is my collection. I gather these things from people that I... help... with their lives, and in return, I sometimes give someone an item, to support them, to get them over a rough time, perhaps."

"I... I don't understand."

Luci picked up something from a nearby table and held it out to Michael. It was a blue jewel about the size of a quarter, set in silver on a long chain. It looked very old. "This is an amulet of Mallici," the man told him, letting the jewel dangle from its chain. "Legend has it that the person who wears this jewel obtains the power to make their most heartfelt desires come true," Luci said softly.

"Really," Michael whispered. He suddenly thought of his own 'heartfelt' desire.

"Here, I want you to have this," Luci said, extending the jewel toward Michael.

"What? No, I can't accept that," though his head was shaking, Michael was not able to take his eyes from the stone. It was a deep, deep blue, with thin lines of gold spider-webbing. It was beautiful.

"Of course you can," the stranger insisted quietly. "I'm giving it to you so you can obtain your heart's desire."

"I... I don't believe in that sort of thing," Michael mumbled. "Besides, I don't have anything to give you in return."

"Oh, I'm sure we could work something out later on," Luci said, his warm smile returning. "Tell you what. You take the stone and wear it for a few days, just to see what happens. If nothing comes out of it, fine, I'll take it back, no problem.

But, if it works... well, isn't it worth taking just on the off chance something *does* happen?"

"Um, sure. Okay," Michael said, slowly reaching out and taking the chain from Luci's hand. He looked at the stone, and the gold veins seemed to pulse in rhythm with his heartbeat. He slipped the chain over his head and put the stone inside his shirt, letting it rest against his bare chest. It felt warm and alive, as if it belonged there. Michael looked up at Luci. "Thank you."

"No need to thank me, son, unless something good comes of it."

"I don't know how I can repay you."

"Don't worry, son, we'll work something out," he told Michael as he walked him back to the entrance.

It was fully dark outside, but a glow of light came from around the corner a few buildings down. "Just go down that way and turn right at the corner," Luci said. "You'll be able to find your way home easily after that."

"All right, thanks again," Michael touched the stone through his shirt.

Luci waived as Michael walked away. When Michael got to the corner, he looked back, but no one was there. Shrugging his shoulders Michael turned the corner, finding himself on a well-lit street, not two blocks from his apartment, with people and cars moving quickly about their business.

He turned back and saw the entrance to an alley just behind him. Looking into the alley, he could see another street at the far end, not more than a hundred yards away. Nowhere in that short alley was there any sign of a strange, dark street filled with unusual, bizarre buildings. Michael rubbed his eyes and looked again, but the scene was the same. He quickly reached up felt for the amulet, relieved to find it still there. At least this is real, he thought and headed home, scratching his head.

#

Early the next morning, Michael was contacted by Carl, one of the concert's producers. It seemed that Mr. Johnson, the opening act for their concert, had choked to death during the evening while eating a celebratory meal. Carl asked if Michael would consider opening for Scott Ireson that night.

At the concert, Michael sang his heart out putting on the performance of his life. The crowd loved him bringing him back for two encores. There happened to be an agent from a west coast record company in the audience that night who was so impressed with Michael's performance he asked to see him after the show and offered Michael a recording contract on the spot. Rinstrom signed, without hesitation.

Michael went on to record over a dozen platinum albums and twice many top ten singles and played several world tours. He was not only famous but had also achieved his heart's desire.

After living his dream for more than twenty years, he decided to retire after the last world tour. Michael ended his last concert with an emotional goodbye speech to his fans, then made his way back to his dressing room, clutching the amulet which had seen him through all the years of success.

Once in his dressing room, he collapsed onto a couch, suddenly exhausted. As he lie his head back against the cushions, he did not notice the amulet and chain slip from around his neck and fall to the floor. Absorbing the surrounding silence, gratefully acknowledging over twenty years of screaming fans and loud music. True, he loved every minute of it, but now, he needed time for himself.

His reverie suddenly broke when a vaguely familiar voice said, "Howdy pardner."

Startled, Michael sat up and saw a tall, lean man dressed all in black, standing in the shadows of the room. He blinked several times until recognition set in. "Luci?" He asked.

The figure stepped forward into the light. "Mr. Rinstrom. It's good to see you again. It's been years."

"Uh, yes. It's good to see you," Michael said, sitting up straightening his shirt, then brushing back his hair somewhat nervously. "I assume you know that the amulet, well, it worked rather well for me," he added, reaching up to touch the stone through his shirt. His fingers fumbled for the amulet but couldn't find it. Michael began to panic, realizing the stone was gone.

"Not to worry, son," Luci said, holding up the chain and amulet for Michael to see. "I've come to collect on our agreement. You remember our agreement, don't ya, son?"

"Oh, sure, I didn't forget. I've thought about that amulet every day since you first gave it to me," Michael said. "For everything I've received these past years, I'll give you anything you want. I can't tell you how happy I've been or how grateful I am."

"Really," Luci said, smiling and moving a little closer to Michael. "Anything I want, eh? I have your word on that?"

"Of course, you have my word. I have more money

than I know what to do with," Michael said and pulled a checkbook and gold pen from the pocket of a coat hanging over the back of a nearby chair. "Just name your price."

“Your soul,” Luci hissed, his face coming close to Michael's.

“Uh, right,” he said, laughing nervously.

Luci's smile quickly vanished, and he grabbed Rinstrom by the throat. "You gave me your word," he hissed as his fingernails dug into Michael's skin.

“I... I plan on keeping my... my word," he struggled to say. "I have millions of dollars."

The smile returned to Luci's face, but there was nothing pleasant about it, this time. He launched Michael across the dressing room with a slight push, and the star crumpled into the corner. "Money," Luci snorted. "I have no need of *money*, but I will take this nice pen of yours,” Luci picked up the gold pen from where it had dropped on the dressing table. “To add to my collection, you know,” he slipped the pen in his pocket.

Stunned, confused, and frightened, Michael sat up and said, "How can you not need money? Everyone needs money."

Luci faced a large mirror over the dressing table slowly removed his tall-crowned hat, revealing a pair of six-inch yellow horns protruding from his greasy black hair, and turned back toward Michael. His dark, deep-set eyes glowed a deep, penetrating red. Rinstrom watched in horror, as Luci's thin face elongated right before his eyes until his chin ended in a sharp point, and his lips drew back to reveal rows of sharpened teeth. "Now, what would the *Devil* need with money?" Luci asked, his voice sounding like the hiss of a large snake.

Pushing himself as far into the corner as he could, Michael moaned, "What... what are you saying?"

Luci moved closer, his long fingers ending with sharpened, yellow nails. "The Devil," he hissed. "What would I, the Devil, need with your useless currency, when I have something much more valuable than mere money?"

As that statement sunk in and Michael began to understand what was happening, he cried, "Noooo!"

"I did my part, son, and you found your dream," Luci hissed and moved closer, his hand reaching out, the yellow claws going for Michael's throat. "Now, it's time to do your part!"

Tears streaming down his face, Michael pushed his back against the wall, but there was no place for him to go. He tried to scream and found that he couldn't, managing to whisper, "Oh, my God!"

Lucifer's fingers closed tightly around Rinstrom's throat, his needle-sharp claws began to draw blood, while he said, "Now you're getting it!"

The End

CAN YOU HEAR ME NOW?

ON A COOL evening in 1955, Edward picked up his longtime girlfriend Christine, from her modest suburban home. He was a twenty-year-old who worked for his grandfather at a local gas station, while was a nineteen-year-old college student. Tonight, they were off to *Mickey's Dinner* for a night of fast food, friends, and fun.

Christine's eyes lit up when Edward pulled into her driveway; how could she not be attracted to his *James Dean* looks. Edward's cherry red, 1946 three quarter ton Chevrolet pickup sputtered as it came to a stop, inside Christine saw Edward had a warm, welcoming smile for her as he stepped out from the driver's side of the vehicle, Christine ran to him and, without hesitation, wrapped her arms firmly around her lover and placed a hungry kiss on his mouth.

"Oh, I missed you, Eddy," Christine said once she had released her embrace.

"I miss you too, sweetie; but it's only been a few days since we saw each other,"

A big smile rose on her lips, and she wrapped her arms around Edward once more saying, "Oh, baby, but it felt like weeks apart."

Christine stared into Edward's eyes with a sultry look. There was a brief moment of silence before Edward asked, "What's going on in that pretty head of yours?"

"I don't think I could live without you in my life... Promise me that you'll never leave me."

"You worry too much, Crissy," Edward responded with a smile of his own.

Christine dropped her arms from around her lover and slowly moped away. Edward quickly realized he had done something wrong; he abruptly ran over to Christine, grabbed her by the arms, and stared hard into her green eyes before he asked, "What? What, did I say that was wrong, Crissy?"

"I was serious about what I said, Edward. I want you to promise me that you'll never leave me."

"Christine Anne Lincoln, I love you more than life itself and *promise* I will never leave you. Even when we are angels at the gates of Heaven, we will continue to be together... Together forever and ever," Edward declared to Christine and then placed a passionate kiss of his own on her lips. "Now, can we go get something to eat? I'm starving."

"Of course," Christine said behind her bright smile.

Edward walked her to the passenger's side of his pickup and opened the door for her.

"After you ma' lady," he said, helping Christine inside.

"Why, thank you, good sir," Christine said in her best mock southern accent.

Edward ran around to the other side of the truck and got into the driver's seat, "Oh, and I hear tonight Mickey his is having a special on Sloppy Joes."

"What is it with you and food, Eddy? You should weigh five hundred pounds with as much as you eat," Christine said, while she watched Edward push the clutch and put the truck into reverse.

"I don't know. I'm just a big fan of good food," he said with a wink.

"All I know is if I eat as much as you, I'd be the size of a hous—"

Christine was interrupted as a speedster viciously collided into the side of Edward's pickup that was halfway out of the driveway. The impact forced Christine into Edward, driving his head through the side window. Blood erupted when shards of glass penetrated his neck. The last thing Christine remembered was when she screamed out...

#

"...Edward!" Christine cried out as she sat up in her bed. Tears traveled the lines of her face; she quickly realized it was a horrible dream about the saddest day in her seventy-four years of life.

"Miss Lincoln are you all right?" An orderly asked rushing into the room.

Christine did not reply right away; she glanced around her tiny nursing home room.

"Y-yes. Yes, my dear, I had a bad dream," Christine muttered.

"Is there anything I can get you?"

"No, no child. Just let me get back to sleep," she replied softly to the young lady in the doorway.

"Okay, Miss Lincoln; if you need anything, don't hesitate to call," the orderly stepped out of the room, closing the door behind her.

Christine lied back down pulling the blankets to her chin and tried to force her thoughts to a happier time, but they continued to return to the night of her lover's tragic death. She thought of the boy who drove the car that killed Edward; his name was Samuel Hanover, who was friends with both Edward and Christine. He was on his way to meet up with them to show off his new '55 Sportster his father bought for him as a graduation present, but as he came upon his friend's old red pickup, Samuel tried to slow down, but the brakes did not work and crashed into his friend's vehicle going fifty miles per hour.

Christine's thoughts returned to her; a telephone, which rested on a side-table next to her bed, began to rang.

Who in the world would call me this time of the night, Christine thought to herself as she reached through the side bed rails to get to the phone.

"Hello?" She answered.

"..."

"Hello?" Christine answered again, but this time with more authority.

"..."

"If you do not answer me right this minute, I'm gonna hang up," Christine demanded.

"...Ur—"

That was the only thing Christine heard before the phone line went dead.

"Damn kids and their prank calls," Christine roared as she slammed the phone down on the receiver. "Don't they realize that old people need to sleep, too?"

Christine heaved a sigh and lay back down; her thoughts ran on how she'd love to deliver punishment to such irreverent juveniles. *If I had had children of my own, they wouldn't have been so disrespectful,* Christine thought to herself.

"They would have been perfect angels." She tugged the blankets back to her chin and rolled over to her side, and thought of what life would have been like with her beloved Edward. A warm comfort covered her at the thought of a different life, a life of happiness, children, and love, and before Christine realized it, she was fast asleep while dreaming of her perfect world.

#

Christine's bloodshot eyes opened to the loud ring of the telephone. She looked at the alarm clock which rested next to the phone; it read *3:31 am*

Christine hissed as she snatched up the receiver and

said, “Hello?”

There was no answer on the other end of the phone line, only a loud static sound. Christine listened for a few moments before she said, "Hello? Can you hear me, hello?"

The line continued to crackle with static. Christine thought she heard a faint voice on the other end of the phone but could not make out what the person had said. Finally, tired, and frustrated, Christine said, "I can't hear you. If this is important, then call back in the morning."

The faint voice lost in the loud static appeared to talk faster, but it was no use. Christine was unable to understand the person and hung up the phone. No sooner did she have the receiver in place atop the telephone's base did it begin to ring once more. The weary older woman lifted the receiver once again and brought it to her ear.

“H-hello," Christine said faintly. Much like before, there was no clear voice, only one drowning in the static. "I can't hear you. Please... please call back in the morning."

The voice in the background did not answer, and the phone line went dead. Christine was concerned that it was an important call; her sister Julianne's health had declined in recent weeks, and perhaps it was bad news that concerned her. Christine called for the young orderly, who walked into her room with a tired smile and warm eyes, "Yes, Miss Lincoln, what do you need, Hun?"

“My dear, has anyone called for me at the Nurse's

station tonight?"

"No, Miss Lincoln, it has been quiet all evening. Not one single phone call," the orderly replied.

Christine sighed in frustration, "Do you know dear if the telephone company can trace a call already made?"

"Yes, they can tell you who made the call, and at what time," the orderly replied.

"Good, in the morning, we will call the phone company and find out who keeps calling me."

"All right, Miss Lincoln, we can do that in the morning, but right now, you need to get some sleep," the orderly said as she stepped out of the room.

"All right, dear. Good night," Christine said. She reached over and picked up the receiver and placed it down next to the base. The old lady smiled inward at the thought of not being disturbed for the rest of the night. "I should've thought of this hours ago."

Christine chuckled to herself at her brilliance lying back down and covering herself up.*Yes, indeed. Should have thought of this earlier.*

#

Several hours later, Christine awoke to the ringing of the telephone. She sat up in bed and stared in bewilderment as the phone rang. Even though the receiver was off the hook it continued to ring. She did not know what to do and thought that perhaps this was all some sort of bizarre dream. But, the old lady knew good and well that she was wide awake.

Finally, Christine gathered enough courage to grab the receiver and brought it up to her ear once again.

“Hello...who is this,” Christine asked, this time her words laced with fear and anxiousness.

The line crackled and popped, but not as loud as it had with the previous calls. Finally, Christine heard someone say, "...You..."

“Say again. You cut out," Christine said.

"...You made— " Then once again, the call dropped, but Christine continued and listened on the phone.

She recognized the voice on the other line and listened intently for him to return to his call. Eventually, after a few moments of waiting, Christine softly spoke into the receiver, "Edward? Eddy, my darling, is that you?"

She waited for a reply, but it did not come. Tired and confused, Christine placed the phone back on the receiver hoping for another call. The old woman sat up in bed staring apprehensively at the small black phone. Her eyes moved to her alarm clock, which read 6:44 am.

There should be people at the phone company by now who can help me, Christine thought to herself as she picked up the entire phone and brought it into bed with her. Christine glared down at the phone for a few more moments before picking up the receiver and placing a call.

“Good morning, this is Ellen. How may I help you today?" The voice on the other end of the line asked.

“Hello? Hello? My name is Christine Lincoln, and I would like to report a problem with the phone line," she said excitedly.

"Okay, Miss Lincoln, what seems to be the problem?"

"Well, I received numerous amounts of phone calls last night, and all I could hear was loud static." She explained. "You see, I don't know who called. It could have been about my sick sister in Washington or... or a dear friend trying to get in touch after all these years."

"I do apologize for that, Miss Lincoln. Let me see what I can do about that," the lady on the other line said as she typed vigorously on her keyboard. "Okay, I can trace the calls that came in for this number last night, but that will take a few moments. Is that all right?"

"Oh yes, dear, that's completely fine," Christine said with a sense of satisfaction. She knew that it would not be much longer until all her questions were to be answered. The old lady sat and listened quietly as the operator clicked away on her keyboard, and then without warning, the clicking stopped.

"That's weird," the lady on the other line said.

"What's that, dear?" asked Christine.

"Well, Miss Lincoln, I was able to locate the origin of the calls...and well, there's no phone service out there," The lady explained with a hint of confusion to her voice.

"So, it's not out of Washington?"

"No, mam, it was made here locally."

"Thank heavens, I was worried it was about my sister," Christine said and then paused for a moment and worked up the nerve and asked her next question.

"Where did the calls come from, dear?"

"Ummm... Miss Lincoln, I don't believe you'd believe me if I told you," the lady on the other line said nervously.

"After the night I just had, dear, try me."

#

It was a warm morning when a bus pulled into a local cemetery. Christine was helped into her wheelchair and then lowered down a hydraulic ramp. Her stomach turned as she glanced around the old graveyard; it brought back many painful memories.

"The last time I was here dear was when we buried my Edward," Christine said to the young orderly who guided her through the cemetery. "That was in 1955...that was over fifty years ago."

The young orderly did not respond but continued to navigate Christine to her desired destination.

Until they came upon a lone headstone that rested beneath a large willow tree.

PICK YOUR ENDING!

If They continue go to page 147

If they stop and do not go any further, go to page 151

MIDDLE OF NOWHERE

"**THEY'RE PLANNING TO** kill every living thing in Manhattan?" Thomas Reyes, the director of Homeland Security, asked after he read through the latest security report. "And we're okay with this?"

"President Alboro is completely ignoring the information that's coming in," replied Kurt Phillips, director of the Central Intelligence Agency.

The two men were inside the Presidential War Room to review all of the latest information gathered on the country's growing terrorist threat. In recent weeks, both agencies had received numerous tips on a certain terrorist group known as the Brotherhood of Humanity. From the information gathered lately, the Brotherhood was making plans to attack Manhattan within a few weeks.

Both directors personally met with the president,

but Alboro turned a deaf ear to their warnings stating that there wasn't enough 'hard' evidence to support such an attack. Now, the two of them needed to decide what would happen next.

"I don't get it," said Thomas, and then threw the report down on the table in front of him. "The Brotherhood of Humanity is based out of England. Why on Earth would they want to attack us here in the States? We've read this damn report at least fifty times, and it still doesn't make any sense why they would do this!"

"Look, Tom," Kurt said as he reached across the table to grab up the report. "We're going to have to bypass the 'why' of this thing and go straight to the 'when.' We need to find out when they plan to carry out this threat."

Thomas sighed. "Next Friday," he stated calmly.

Kurt slowly looked up from the report and stared at him. "What?"

Reyes got up from his chair and walked around the table to where Kurt stood. "My God, you really are an ignorant bastard, aren't you?" he asked quietly. "Friday, Kurt. They plan to attack next Friday!"

Phillips sank into a chair stunned by what he heard, and the room was silent for several heartbeats. He placed his hands on the table and began to tap his fingers on the highly polished surface.

Finally, Phillips looked up at Thomas. "How do you know this?" he asked.

"I have the uncensored version," he replied and smiled slightly.

Kurt jumped to his feet and slammed his fist down on the table. "Uncensored! Are you telling me there are two freaking versions of this report?"

"Calm down, Kurt. There's nothing to get excited about."

"Christ, Thomas! I'm the director of the bleeding C.I.A., and I get a god damned edited version of the report?"

"We thought it would be for the best," Reyes replied, with a shrug of his shoulders.

"We? Who the Hell is we?" demanded Kurt, as he slammed his fist down on the table once again and glared up at the other man.

"How long have we been working on this?" Thomas asked. "Three, maybe four months now, and you still haven't figured it out? Don't you get it, Kurt; they don't want you to stop this. They're the ones orchestrating the whole thing!"

"And who the hell are 'they?'" Kurt asked softly, and his voice shook slightly.

"That, my poor friend is something you will never know," Reyes replied, as he pulled a 9mm semi-automatic out from under his coat and pointed it at him. "You just couldn't leave well enough alone, could you? No, you had to keep poking your nose into things and now..." Thomas cocked the gun, "...you die."

#

Friday Morning. 0640, E.S.T.

"Mother Goose, this is Father Time. The pack is

nearing the target. Over," Major Wall said as his group of X-9 Bombers streaked toward their objective.

"Copy that, Father Time. What is your E.T.A., over?" the small, faint voice asked from Major Wall's headset.

"Mother Goose, our E.T.A. is thirty minutes. We're awaiting your orders. Over," the major said as he started his final systems check.

"Father Time, drop airspeed to mach one and bring altitude down to six thousand feet for a bombing run. Over."

"Copy that, Mother Goose," the major responded. "Father Time, out."

#

0650, E.S.T.

As dawn broke over the city, Victoria Sinclair rushed around her modest, three-bedroom townhome as she tried to collect the items her son needed while he dressed for school.

"Jason, are you about ready?" she called as she pulled her son's notebook out from under a cushion of the couch.

"Yeah, Momma. I just need my jacket," Jason replied and then poked his head out from behind his bedroom door.

"Well, come on. We don't want to be late," Victoria stuffed a sandwich into a small, brown paper bag. As she closed the bag, she heard the sound of her six-year-old coming down the hall.

"Momma, today's show and tell. Can I take Teddy to

school?" Jason held up his little bear.

"'May' I take Teddy to school," she corrected him. "And, yes, but you take good care of him. Your daddy got you that bear just before he..."

Jason gave his mother a sobering look. "Heaven, momma," her son said. "He went to Heaven. I'll take good care of Teddy. I promise."

After Victoria gave her son a quick embrace, they left the townhouse, where they met the city's milling morning pedestrians on the crowded sidewalk. Victoria stood there a moment, her mind still treasuring the memory of her late husband, until she heard her son shout.

"Catch me if you can!" She looked up in time to see him dart off down the street.

"Hey. Get back here," Victoria called out with a smile and began to give chase.

#

0710, E.Ṣ.T.

"Mother Goose, this is Father Time. We are approaching the target area, awaiting the go-ahead order. Over," Major Wall said as the bombers swooped in over the ocean with the sun at their backs. He looked out at the skyline of Manhattan.

"Father Time, this is Mother Goose. You have a Green Light for the mission. I repeat, you are 'Go' for the drop," replied the man at the other end of the major's transmission.

"Roger that, Mother Goose. Father Time, over and

out," the major said and switched to the in-flight frequency. "Okay, boys, we've got a 'signal green.' Let's send these bastards to Hell!" he said. A small button was pushed several seconds later, which released two 500-pound bombs from his plane onto the city below, and a dozen more bombs screamed away after them.

THE LEFTOVERS

I DECIDED TO write my daily events in this journal. Maybe it will help subside the nightmares. But let's face it; what I now do for a living is no picnic. Sure, maybe being the Cable Guy wasn't as glamorous as a job as, say, a computer technician—but it was a paying job nonetheless, and boy, do I miss that job.

This morning, when we all pulled up to that day's worksite, it was just barely dawn. I got out of the truck; the stench of rotting flesh filled the air. It had been three weeks since that scientist from Long Island created the cure for what was called the Zombie Flu. I mean, sure, we'd all heard of the Bird Flu, the pig flu, and Hell, at one point, there was even a seal flu!

But the new strain of influenza only affected the poor souls, who (for the lack of a better word) were already dead. Somehow, this "Zombie Flu" actually raised the dead and gave them a big appetite for flesh. I know what you're thinking, and no, they didn't come up from their graves and wander around, saying, "Brains!"

How realistic is that? I mean, yeah, I believed what the bible said about the dead will rise again, although that wasn't quite what I had in mind. Anyway, perhaps the dead who were already entombed became reanimated as well, but we'll never know. Let's face it, gentle reader, if they did, in fact, come back to life, how in the Hell were they going to get out of their coffins? Those suckers were sealed airtight and crafted from some sort of metal—there was no getting out of those bad boys.

I'm talking about the people in the morgue who hadn't received an autopsy. They were the ones who came back and raised some hell with us livin' folks. But, enough with the history lesson, you probably already know what went down if you're reading this.

So back to my job. I was hired by the Feds to help clean up what they called "The Leftovers." Once infected by the Zombie Flu and treated by the military or militia, the bodies were organized by civilians to aid the Feds. And as you can guess, after eleven months of the flu, there were a lot of Leftovers.

Sunup to sundown, the crew and I drive out to certain locations where Leftovers were spotted. We pick up the bodies and disinfect the area with a high-powered sprayer. I know, fun job, right? But hell, we're paid by the Feds, which in turn means big bucks; they even put some of us who lost our homes during the decontamination stage up in nice cabins (which were most of us). Today, we all headed out to Apple Valley toward the Happy Trails Highway (no, really, I'm not making this up). It was named after a former song resident and legendary film star, Roy Rogers, who sang in his movies. Anyway, it was still somewhat dark when we got there, but the weather was already uncomfortable. Once I got out of the truck, I looked out at the road in front of us; it was covered with Leftovers. The desert sun had cooked the corpses, and the smell of death was everywhere.

We started to load Leftovers into the back of our truck; it was another fun-filled day as usual. During lunch, we all tried to get something to eat; well, everyone other than Martin. Martin came from the south, namely Arkansas. His family died during the flu, and he decided to come out west and eventually joined us in the cleanup crew.

Every day during lunch, Martin scavenged the area and lifted the wallets from the Leftovers' pockets. We'd all told Martin several times over that the money he found was useless since the Bank of China now backed our money. He always smiled and told us he knew as he grabbed up another wallet.

But today, today was different. While we gobbled down our sandwiches, Martin decided to check abandoned buildings for more Leftovers. You couldn't blame the poor bastard; it was the last days of August and at one hundred and four degrees out—I wouldn't want to stay out in the heat either. I watched as Martin walked into building after building; he held the wallets out in front of him and dropped them in a pile in front of an old *Walgreen's* to our left.

Martin always put his findings in a pile, and right before the end of lunch, he decontaminated them with the pressure hose. What a waste of time, I thought to myself as I watched him quickly go in and out of a building. But, hell, now that I think of it, that was what made him happy. Martin didn't have any friends or family to go home to, so if counting useless money made him happy and gave him the drive to get out of bed in the morn, then good for him.

I had finished my sandwich when Martin walked into another building. I glanced at the pile of wallets and noted he was having a good day as his mountain made from leather rose twice as high as usual by the end of lunch.

Martin was in the building for about five minutes or less when he ran out screaming. A Leftover clung to his back and appeared to bite at his neck and shoulder continuously. Martin collapsed to his knees, and three more infected ran out of the building and attacked him as well.

The others and I ran to the truck grabbing our rifles. We fired on the Leftovers making our way to Martin. By the time the three of us made it, he was on his back covered in his own blood. I looked down at him and gave him a weak smile.

I told Martin he was going to be all right, and we'd get him help. Martin frowned and said: "They took my hand," he showed me his bloody stump.

Martin's breaths became labored, and his eyes rolled

into his head. I told him to stay with us. His eyes focused on me one last time, and he told me: "Wallets. Please finish. At my home. Please."

His body went limp. I wept for Martin. He was a simple and kind person and didn't deserve to die like that. I held him for a few moments and told him to go be with his family.

After the attack on Martin, we agreed to call it a day. I washed the wallets and took them with us as we headed home. No one said a word until we got home when one of the guys said: "Poor Martin."

It took me until after dinner to muster the strength to enter Martin's room. I'd never been in there before. It was a small room, with a bed over by the wall and a fan located at the foot. I noticed there was a wastebasket next to the door. It was full of odds and ends junk, but mainly filled with currency.

At first, I wondered why Martin kept the money he found in the trash, but I answered my own question as I walked inside. The wall next to the door was covered with wallet-sized pictures. I scanned over the unknown people, but they were all the same. Each wore a smile and appeared to be happy with life. The scenes were different. There was one black and white picture that stood out to me. A man who appeared to be in his thirties or forties stood next to a young boy. They were outside and next to a barbecue—they too looked happy.

Then, something caught my eye. A birthmark was located on the boy's cheek; it was the same as the one Martin had. I took the picture off the wall, flipped it over, and read:

Pops (43) and Martin (12) 1969.

I placed the picture back on the wall and sat on the side of Martin's bed. I took the photos from each wallet and tossed the rest in the trash. One by one, I carefully placed the photographs in the blank spots on the wall. A little time later, I had filled all the open areas with the new pictures. There was only one empty spot left. I stared at the uncovered piece of the wall for a few moments.

Eventually, I got out my wallet and thumbed through my own photos and pulled out one picture of my family, and I. Giving it a small kiss I placed it in the last open space on the wall. It was a perfect fit. I couldn't help but smile as I turned off the light and stepped out of his room.

The End

HELLUVA TIME

ALFREDO VEGA LIED on his death bed in his home located amid the rolling hills of Colombia. His family filled the ill man's room and watched in sorrow as he fought for his final few breaths. Vega was the head of the Colombian Cartel that shipped most of its cocaine to the United States.

He waved his priest over and had the holy man sit down beside him. "Father, please…" Vega said weakly. "I must have confession. I am responsible for many bad things, and I must be forgiven before I die so that I can make it to Heaven."

"Go ahead, my son, I am here for you," the priest said to Alfredo and began the routine of confession.

"Forgive me, Father, for I have sinned; it has been seven years since my last confession," Vega said. "I have personally taken the life of nine men and was responsible for hundreds, if not thousands more. I have taken the Lord's name in vain more times than I can remember. I have slept with every woman in this house out of wedlock. Including Sister Roberta—boy, she was a fine piece of—"

"Go on, my son, is there more?" the priest interrupted.

"I have stolen more than I can recall, and I have done more drugs than thought humanly possible. I've lied, at least twenty times a day and …and I think that's it, Father."

"All right, my son; five Hail Mary's and– oh, crap." Before the priest could finish, Alfredo Vega had taken his last breath.

#

When Vega opened his eyes, he found himself in Las Vegas. The former Colombian Drug King was dressed in a white suit with a matching white fedora.

"I'm in Las Vegas? How in the Hell did I get here?" he asked.

A stranger stopped in front of Vega. "That's it," he said, "you got the right idea." Then he walked away.

Alfredo was confused; how could he be in the United States and healthy? Only minutes ago, he was knocking on death's door back at his home in Colombia.

He grabbed the next passerby. "Where in the Hell am I?" he asked.

The man grinned and exposed small, sharp teeth.

"Yes, Hell," he replied.

"I don't understand. What do you mean?" Vega asked as he let go of the stranger. The sharp-toothed man's grin transformed into an evil smile as he pointed to a sign which read:

WELCOME TO FABULOUS HELL!

The man patted Vega on the shoulder. "Welcome to your ever after," and then he walked away. Alfredo stood there on the busy street of Hell and realized that he died before the priest could finish his confession. "That stupid bastard let me die and go to Hell!"

"Oh, Hell's not that bad, Alfredo. There's so much fun stuff to do around these parts," someone said spoke behind him. He quickly turned around and saw a tall black man dressed in a blood-red suit with a matching hat. He reminded Vega of a pimp from the 1970s.

"Who are you?" Alfredo asked.

"Oh, yeah, I'm Roland. Welcome to Hell, Alfredo. Sorry, I'm late; I had an early suicide– you know how teens are nowadays."

"How do you know my name?" Alfredo asked although he was afraid to learn the answer.

"No need to trip, my man. I'm your one and only guardian demon."

"Guardian Demon?"

"Yeah, you know, whatever the "G" man has up there, the boss has down here. I've been watching over you your whole life, dawg," Roland said with a smile that showed off his pearly white and glistening gold teeth.

"Wait a minute... you're a demon? I thought demons were ugly and frightening."

"This is just a cover, Al—I can call you Al, right?" Roland asked, but before Alfredo could answer, he continued. "Good. Anyway, so this is a cover. You know the boss was trying to get more newcomers, so we changed things up. You should have seen this place before the remodeling; what a pit, I'll tell ya."

"So, you're saying that you are some hideous demon underneath your skin?" Vega asked.

"Shh, Son, I'm so scary; just one look at me and you'd piss yourself just like when you were nine," Roland said and then paused for an answer from Vega, but only got an amused look. "Oh, come on, dawg, you remember when you were nine? Okay, okay. You were watching some horror movie, and it frightened you so bad you wet yourself."

Alfredo stood there for a moment and thought about what he had heard. "Nope," he finally said. "Don't recall that one. Must have been someone else, amigo."

"What? Don't you remember that? Your scared ass pissed your mom's new couch, and you were so embarrassed you blamed it on the dog."

"Oooh."

"Yeah, that's right, now you remember. Anyway, I'd make you piss yourself like that."

"Oh."

"Aw, come on, Al, it was a long time ago." Roland

put an arm over Vega's shoulders, and they started to walk down the strip.

"So, you said that there were a lot of things to do here in Hell?" Alfredo asked.

"Yeah, there sure are," Roland answered as they came up to a set of apartment buildings. "That's why you're here."

"What's this place?" Alfredo asked.

"This is your new home; go freshen' up. We have a party to attend tonight."

"What party? We're going to have a party because I arrived today?"

"Na, today's just Monday," he replied but received a blank look. "Oh, I forgot to tell you. Every day we have a different mandatory thing to do around here. It's kinda like our jobs, but it's fun and how we make our livings. Today is Monday, so we all have to go party for eight hours."

Later that day, Roland took Alfredo to where all the events were held, and for the first day, they partied and danced for eight evil hours. Afterward, they had the rest of the day to do whatever they wanted. Vega could not believe how much he enjoyed being in Hell.

On the second day, the demon and Alfredo headed back to where the events were held. "So, Al, do you like to drink, my friend?" Roland asked.

"Yeah, of course, why?"

"Well, that's what we are going to do today. We are going to drink until we puke, and then we'll drink some more."

"Right on, amigo. I am one who can hold his booze,"

Vega said with a smile.

And the two did just that; they drank and drank until they puked, and then they drank some more until the eight hours were up. And again, once the eight hours were up, they were free to do whatever they pleased. On the third day, Alfredo spent eight hours smoking the finest cigars imported from Cuba. He enjoyed himself so much that he put in a little overtime. After all, he wasn't worried about dying of cancer—he was already dead. On Thursday, Alfredo arrived to find a wide variety of drugs: cocaine, speed, smack, weed, and crack. But of course, Alfredo was a coke man; he did so much he almost felt like he was back home.

Vega and Roland decided to share a crack pipe before calling it a day, and as the two sat there, Alfredo couldn't help but reflect on his last four days in Hell.

He had had so much fun; he would never have believed it possible. Afterward, Alfredo and Roland walked back to the apartment buildings. "So," Vega said, "I have to ask, just because I had so much fun these last four--all day the smoking, the drinking, the drugs. What can possibly be better than that?"

"Well, you're gay, right?" Roland asked with an evil smile.

"No, I'm straight," Vega snapped back at the demon.

"Oh, then you're not going to like tomorrow at all, dawg."

The End

CHRONICLING THE END

Observation Unit

EARLY, ON A Saturday morning in January, while most slept comfortably in their beds, two physicists were busy on their latest project. For these two men, their day started hours ago.

"Steady…steady now," Mark Williamson said in a shaky voice as he peered through a high-powered microscope.

"Relax, Mark, I'm in complete control," Xavier Scott said with a confident grin. At the same time, he continued to look through his own microscope.

"Would you please explain *again* exactly how adding two extra Hydrogen molecules into a cell infected with influenza is going to become a cure against the flu?"

Williamson watched as Scott began to place a single molecule into the cell.

“It's basic biology, Mark. Suppose we add two molecules of Hydrogen to the outer shielding of the cell. In that case, it will not be able to create a covalent bond with the cell infected with influenza," he explained. Scott paused for a moment and looked up from his microscope. "If we employ this method and inject it into everyone, then they'll have a *natural* immunity because the virus won’t be able to make a bond with their own cells.”

“My only concern, Xavier, is we do not know how the cell will react. No one’s ever tried this.”

“Shhh!” Xavier said softly. “Okay, enough chitchat. I need to concentrate.”

His hand trembled as he inserted the first of two molecules contained in a small hypodermic syringe. Scott gave Mark Williamson a hand gesture to turn on the overhead microphone. Williamson leaned in and pushed a small button off to his left. There was a loud *click,* and Xavier began to speak.

“Beginning test number one. Xavier Scott lead engineer, along with Mark Williamson, as safety. I am inserting the first needle now."

Williamson spoke up. “The contents of the syringe are one positively charged Hydrogen particle protected with one unit of normal saline containing zero-point nine percent of Sodium Chloride.”

Scott looked up from the microscope as sweat formed across his brow and traveled down his face. “All right, specimen one is in. Now we wait for the bond to be made with the infected cell,” he said, and then wiped the sweat away with his lab coat sleeve.

"Check to see if the covalent bond has been made," Williamson said impatiently. "It only takes nanoseconds to create if it works right."

"Okay. The first examination after the initial injection…there has, in fact, been a covalent bond made with the cell. We will ready the next specimen shortly."

Scott waved his hand to signal Williamson to stop the recording.

"Do you want me to get the other syringe ready, Xavier?"

"No. I need a smoke. Let's take five and meet back here at One-Fifteen."

"Okay. Sounds like a plan."

#

Megan sat on the edge of an examination table as she waited for the physician to return with her cardiac test results. She was a twenty-four-year-old personal trainer who always believed her body was in perfect condition.

That was until she collapsed in the gym a week ago while on a treadmill. By the time the paramedics arrived, Megan had not only slipped into unconsciousness, but she stopped breathing as well.

Her doctor believed the incident was caused by dehydration and fatigue, but he recommended Megan follow up with a cardiologist to make sure. The following week she met with Dr. Harris, who, in turn, asked her to participate in several basic tests to examine the cardiac muscle.

As Megan awaited the test results, she thought about her current situation. She knew that heart disease ran in her family but always felt that it was some sort of old wives' tale. *Surely people cannot inherit a bad heart,* she thought.

A soft knock broke her reverie, and Dr. Harris walked into the room; he held a folder with Megan's name written on it. At first, the physician did not speak. Instead, he pulled up a chair and reviewed the contents inside the folder.

Megan felt her heart race with anticipation; she could not wait any longer and broke the silence. "Well?" she asked.

"Well, Ms. Tunner…there's never an easy way to say this," the doctor said without looking up from the folder. "So, I will be straight forward with you."

"Please do."

"All right, then. Have you ever heard of Cardiomyopathy?"

"Cardioma—what?"

"Cardiomyopathy. To state it simply, it is a serious disease in which the heart muscle becomes inflamed and doesn't work as well as it should."

Dr. Harris finally glanced up from the folder and met her eyes for the first time. Megan heaved a hard sigh as she tried to process what the doctor just told her.

"So, do I have it?"

"I'm afraid you do, Ms. Tunner."

He averted his eyes and returned his attention to the folder.

"Okay…okay, what now then? I mean, what's the cure?"

Dr. Harris looked up from the folder, shook his head, and stared at Megan with a grim expression. "I'm sorry, child, but there is no known cure for cardiomyopathy."

"Okay…all right…so, what's the treatment then," Megan asked in a broken and shaky voice. "I don't want to die."

"Well, I can place you on digoxin and some Lasix to help fight against heart failure. But with your age coming into play," he said softly. " Megan... because you're so young, I recommend we get you signed up on a heart transplant list."

#

The silence was deafening in the lab. The only sound heard was Williamson's heavy respirations as he extracted the molecule from the vial's liquid into a small syringe. When the substance filled the syringe, he slowly handed it over to his lab partner.

Once Xavier held the syringe in hand, he used his other hand to adjust the microphone that descended from the ceiling and then gave Williamson the signal to begin recording.

"Beginning phase two of test one. The first Hydrogen implanted into the cell created a covalent bond as planned."

He leaned into the binoculars of the microscope and gently placed the needle of a syringe onto the surface of the petri dish. Xavier slid the syringe forward with methodical slowness toward the cell wall and then began to inject the molecule.

"I am now placing the second Hydrogen molecule into the infected specimen. If your theory is correct, then the particle should connect as happened with the first, therefore forcing the infected elements from the cell."

"Thus, creating the greatest cure known to man," Williamson said with a slight chuckle. But his mood quickly altered when he noticed Xavier's expression. "What? What's wrong?"

Xavier Scott looked up from his microscope with a remorseful look, though he did not directly answer Williamson's question. Everything they had worked on—all of the studies and reports that the two completed—and the final experiment was a complete failure. "I… I'm sorry, Mark… it's not taking," Scott finally said as he looked down at the microscope in front of him.

"Well…what, I mean…uh…what's the problem?"

"The second molecule…it's not active, Mark. It's just floating there—the damned thing isn't creating a bond."

Xavier walked away from the microscope. He came to a stop a few steps later, as if uncertain whether he should walk or speak. Xavier paused for a moment and then rushed back toward Mark and the lab table.

"FUCK!" Xavier screamed. "Two years of work

flushed down the godforsaken drain! I need some air. I'll be right back."

Mark nodded and stepped back as Xavier rushed past him.

"I don't believe this shit!" Xavier said as he kicked out at a trashcan. The metallic cylinder shot across the lab and crashed into a metal tray of unused specimens.

"Xavier, watch out! That's our last batch of specimens. We can't afford to get more!"

"Specimens? Who gives a rat's ass about them? The experiment is *over*. We were wrong; got it?"

"But perhaps that second one was from a bad batch? Maybe we co—"

"No, no!" Xavier interrupted. "It came from the same damn batch as the first one. If it were a bad batch, then the first molecule wouldn't have made the bond."

"Look…all I'm saying is let's try another batch. That is if you didn't destroy all of them."

"All right." Xavier bent down to grab an undamaged vial which lied at his feet. He snatched up the container and examined it for a moment. "Fine. You really want to continue the project, even though we both now know it's a failure?"

"This is where we belong, Xavier." Williamson stood next to a microscope and gestured at it. "We all fail once in a while."

"I don't fail!"

Xavier threw the vial toward Williamson. The vial flew past Williamson and crashed into the microscope, which caused a small but powerful explosion on the petri dish they were working on.

"Mark!" Xavier screamed in fear.

A thick white cloud instantly filled the lab's chamber, and though Xavier could not see his partner, he was certain that the force of the reaction drove Williamson to the floor. The room became silent; the only thing that could be heard was a *sizzling* sound.

Lost in a white blankness, Xavier Scott knew he needed to get the hell out of that lab. Slowly he began to make his way to the left—the scientist knew that was where the exit was. But before Scott could get to the door, he came to a sudden halt.

What about Mark, he thought. In all the commotion, his first thoughts went to his needs, but what about his partner?

Xavier needed to know if Williamson was all right. He paused for a moment as he pondered his options. Finally, Scott called out to his friend. "Mark!" He waited for a moment for a possible response. There was nothing.

Xavier frantically continued to search for the exit as he stumbled through the thick smoke. *Where is that damned door?*

He moved blindly along the lab until his foot brushed against something soft. The young scientist stood motionless for a moment.

"M-mark? Mark, is that you?" he asked.

There was no answer. The only thing the scientist heard was a faint moan. Xavier leaned over and waved his hand back and forth in search of whatever he brushed against.

As Xavier searched, he heard a pain-filled moan,

and followed the noise until his hand came in contact with Williamson's shoe, which he could just barely see. The cries became louder at his touch, and a noticeable stench of burnt flesh wafted in the haze.

"It's okay, buddy," Xavier said and moved closer to his friend. "It's all right…I'm here."

Again, the only response was a low-toned groan. This time it sounded a bit different—it almost sounded *angry*. Scott could finally see Williamson, gasping at what he saw. His friend and longtime lab partner had suffered severe burns to his entire body, which transformed him into something monstrous. What especially caught Xavier's attention was his friend's eyes—they were a yellowish-orange color.

"What in *God's* name?" Williamson attempted to move, but Xavier intervened. "Relax. Try not to move. I'm going to get help. Do you hear me, Mark? I"m going to get you some help."

"Uaaah…" came Williamson's reply.

"All right, buddy, I'll be right ba—"

Xavier was interrupted when Williamson's monstrous hand grabbed his throat. The grasp became unbelievably tight and quickly cut off Scott's oxygen flow. The moans now sounded like growls.

Xavier tried to speak, but that was useless. Scott's dull and lifeless yellowed eyes, come closer through the haze. Smoke rose from his friend's back. Scott opened his mouth to scream realizing Williamson meant to bite him. As as his partner's teeth neared his face, Xavier desperately clawed at Williamson's hand on his throat, but incisors bit into his cheek scraping bone. Hot blood flowed down his neck. Pain exploded as Scott sheared off a chunk of facial meat and began to chew.

#

It was Saturday afternoon when Megan Tunner tried to answer her phone. Not entirely awake, she picked up the receiver on the first ring.

"Hello?"

"Megan?" A man's voice asked. "Megan Tunner?"

"This is she…who is this?"

"Miss Tunner, my name is Emanuel. I'm from Doctor Mukundray Patel's office."

"Yeah. Okay." Megan could barely focus. "What can I do for you?"

"Actually, it's what we can do for you. We have a match for your heart transplant."

The words stunned her. "What? I mean…seriously? This fast?"

"I would not joke about the seriousness of this matter. Dr. Patel, had me contact you to see if you could meet him at the hospital by five?"

"Well…yes—of course," she stammered as her heart pounded.

"Very good then. We will see you at five."

#

A clock on the wall read five minutes until six o'clock. Megan had anxiously waited to see the doctor for almost an hour. Worry and fear begin to set in. *What if something's wrong? Am I going to get my new heart?* Many questions raced through her mind, and fear pumped through her.

Her mind was set at ease when she heard someone speak outside her room. "Good evening, Dr. Patel."

"Hello," came another voice from behind the closed door. "How are you today?"

Megan leaned closer to the door to eavesdrop on the conversation.

"I'm good, thank you. O.R. One is prepped and ready for your next case."

"Yes, very good. Who's next on the list?"

"Megan Tunner, a twenty-four-year-old with Cardiomyopathy."

"Oh, yes! I remember her. She is a fortunate girl, you know?"

"Why is that, doctor?"

"She has been on the list for less than a month, and with a double O-negative blood type—well, it did not look too promising."

"So, you found a double O-negative match then?"

"Yes, there was a lab accident in Barstow, and one of the men was a donor, remarkably with her blood type."

Once the doorknob began to turn, Megan pulled back and sat up in her chair. A man walked into her room, a short Indian, very well-groomed. He wore a bleached white lab coat and had an equally bleached smile.

"Hello, Miss Tunner. I am Dr. Patel. I will be doing your operation this evening."

"Hello, doctor," she muttered.

"Do you have any questions?" the doctor asked with a blunt demeanor.

"No…no, I don't think so."

"Ah, very good. Then I will see you in the operating room."

The no-nonsense doctor walked out of the room and left Megan with a hopeful smile.

#

After seven hours on the operating table, orderlies wheeled Megan Tunner into the recovery room. Dr. Patel spoke to his colleagues. "The operation itself was successful—now if only her body does not reject the heart."

A couple of hours after surgery, Megan took a turn for the worse. The nurse on duty noted that her skin appeared a dusky gray and that Megan's heart rate was up to one hundred eighty-six. She feared that the new heart was being rejected, so the nurse called Dr. Patel.

By the time the doctor arrived, he had found that Megan was not only detached from all life support, but she also was not even in her bed. He saw his patient crouched on the floor next to her bed, her back toward Dr. Patel.

"Miss Tunner? Are you all right? What is going on here?" he demanded.

She did not reply to his question or even acknowledge his presence.

"Miss Tunner—Megan, where is your nurse?" Patel

asked as he slowly moved to where Megan was crouched on the floor, and as he got closer, he heard her struggle for breath.

"Are you having trouble breathing? I think it best we put you back on the breathing machine."

Again, no answer. The doctor began to think that she was having an allergic reaction to a sedative. As he walked up to her, Patel placed his hand on the back of her head.

"Megan, do you hear me? I think—" He was unable to finish his sentence. As his hand slid down her scalp, her skin detached from the skull and flipped over in his hand. He gazed at the backside of her scalp and the hair hanging from his splayed fingers. He felt his breaths come in short gasps, and he wheezed out a short prayer.

Patel backed away from her standing for several moments until Megan turned to face him. The doctor covered his mouth to keep from retching. Skin began to peel from her face, her yellow eyes glowed; contrasting against the neon lighting. Patel squealed when he saw a half-eaten finger dangle from her teeth, frozen with fright, standing in total disbelief at the monstrosity that crouched before him. In that instant, he was horrified by the thought, that before him, crouched the future of humanity.

She expelled a monstrous hiss and exposed bloodstained teeth, her legs tensed to leap. Patel attempted to flee, but the only thing that made it to the door was a river of blood.

CIRCUS, CIRCUS

BLOOD DRIPPED FROM a blade onto the hotel carpet as the murderer crept down a hallway with individual rooms on either side. The man who held the blood-covered blade was freakishly tall and muscular. He wore a pair of tattered overalls and a patterned flannel shirt. His greasy long curly hair hung over a clown mask; the mask itself covered the murderer's face but exposed the rest of his head.

The killer moved slowly until he saw a door to one of the rooms, stood slightly open. With each step he took toward the room, his pace increased with the excitement of a child Christmas morning when they saw all their presents under the tree.

He drove his foot into the door; that erupted into splinters from the force of his kick. The man moved into the room, which was dark and quiet—hearing only his heart as it raced. Standing in the center of the room he listened for any sound. Without warning, he turned to one of the beds and drove the long-bloodstained blade through the mattress. A squeal came from under the bed, and the killer could not help but smile.

He tugged on the blade hearing the sound of impact against the carpet. The madman saw fresh blood on the knife as it came out of the mattress; he brought the metal closer and ran a dirty finger down the blood-coated blade. The killer examined the blood with homicidal ecstasy that was dampened when he heard a sound coming from beneath the bed.

Grabbing the metal frame he heaved it upwards exposing a man convulsing wildly. Without any thought, remorse, or sympathy, the killer swung his weapon severing the man's head from his body. Blood erupted from where the skull once sat atop the torso and quickly pooled on the floor.

He knelt down grabbing the decapitated head by the hair to examine the victim's face letting out an evil laugh confirming his victim's identity—to be the man he'd come for.

#

George Laimbeer was a simple man having no big dreams. What he really wanted Laimbeer, already had. A good job as a mechanic, a nice home, and, most importantly, a beautiful wife. The couple recently moved from New Mexico to Las Vegas, for a better opportunity to find work. George's wife Lydia was the driving force behind the relocation; she was a real estate agent, but sales were dramatically down since the stock market plummeted in 2008.

Lydia convinced George that Vegas real estate was *hot* and genuinely believed that she'd have a better chance to make good money there. But for Laimbeer, he didn't care where the two of them lived, as long as they were together.

George knew he wasn't the smartest man to walk the planet, but he knew a good thing when he saw one. Lydia was definitely a *good* thing. She was a cheerleader in high school, Miss Albuquerque, while in college, and Laimbeer lusted after her the entire time. He knew that he was a lucky man to be with her and would do anything to keep it that way.

Lydia got a job with a real estate company catering to high priced clientele, and in her first week on the job, she made more money than George would bring home in a month. To some men, that would have been a problem, but Laimbeer couldn't have had been happier.

Even so, the happiness began to fade as the days turned to weeks that transformed into months. Lydia spent less time at home and more time with her clients. George's imagination began to get away from him. Laimbeer decided to confront his wife when she got home, despite any pain the truth would cause, he had to know what was going on.

#

Glancing up at the clock on the wall when he saw the headlights of his wife's car coming into the driveway. It was 2:00 AM. *How could she be selling houses at two in the damn morning?* Laimbeer sat back into a wooden rocking chair and patiently waited for Lydia to come inside.

She stepped into the house softly closing the door behind her walking through the dark house when she heard him speak.

"Working late, dear?"

"What…are you still doing up?" Lydia stammered, flipping on the lights in the living room to find George in the rocking chair looking exhausted and pale with dark circles under each eye. "George, is something the matter?"

A faint grin appeared before Laimbeer leaned forward and rested his forearms on his knees. He stared down at the floor for some time never looking up at her. "How long have you been having an affair?" he eventually asked.

"Wha—I, uh...," was all Lydia got out of her mouth.

"Just tell me the truth, Lydia," Laimbeer said sternly.

"Why do you think that, George?" Lydia asked. She walked over to where Laimbeer sat kneeling beside him. His wife placed her hand gently atop his. Upon feeling her touch, George looked at his love and saw the pain he'd caused, in her eyes. In that instant, Laimbeer realized that he had been a fool to question Lydia's loyalty to him.

"I'm sorry, my love, I should not have questioned you. It's just that you work so much, and I never see you anymore. I—," he paused for a moment and arranged his thoughts. "I jumped to a conclusion. Please forgive me."

Lydia gave George a warm smile and stared into his eyes before she told him, "Of course I will. I'll tell you what; I closed on a home for that big casino owner. He gave me a week of rooms for free at his new casino—the one that has a circus theme. Let's take next week off and have a small vacation?"

She saw the life return into George's tired eyes.

"Okay, let's do it," he said.

#

The following Monday, the Laimbeers arrived at the newly opened hotel and casino. George thought it was insane to have a circus-inspired casino, but he was with Lydia for an entire week, and that was all that mattered. He felt horrible accusing his wife of cheating, promising that he'd make up for it while they were at the hotel.

On the first day, George and Lydia agreed to play tourist, and went to a show. It was a corny magic act, but George appeared to enjoyed it. That evening the couple dinned at the casino's most expensive restaurant and ending the day with a few hours at the slots. It was a picture-perfect day, and neither of them could have had asked for a better one.

Lydia and George ended the night with a the

passionate exploration of each other Lydia taking notice of how intense her husband was, something that had been missing for some time, and she prayed it would never disappear again.

#

It was a few minutes past midnight when George opened his eyes; his wife was fast asleep, but he was restless. Laimbeer lied there for a while, thinking. Unable to sleep he decided to take a walk. George got out of bed, kissing his wife on the forehead, threw on his clothes and out of his hotel room.

Laimbeer turned away from the door, gasping with fear as a giant of a man wearing a clown mask over his face, stood in front of him. George shrieked as the clown's blade was thrust at him. He turned and tried to run but was stopped as when the weapon's tip entered his back tearing out the front of his arm.

George collapsed in pain while he cried out for mercy. "Please!" Laimbeer begged, but the man paid no attention and continued to swing his blade. The injured man held up his hands to protect his face, but the force of the swing went through his hands slicing his cheek. Upon seeing several of his fingers lying in a puddle of blood at his knees, George screamed.

With no sign of emotion, the masked man stood before Laimbeer enjoying his cried of pain and uncontrollable weep in fear. The man stepped back from Laimbeer and brought his blade up for another strike, but he stopped when a robust masculine voice shouted from behind them. "Hey! Hey, what the hell you think you're doing?"

The masked man turned in the voice's direction finding a younger man about George's height, and exceptionally well built who ran toward the masked clown. Before he could do anything, the killer brought the knife down on top of the young man's head splitting his skull in two. George watched in terror as the man fell lifeless to the ground. While the killer's back was turned, George quickly got to his feet and ran away as fast as his shaky legs would carry him.

#

Twenty minutes after midnight Lydia awoke and found George was not beside her and sat at the end of the bed. She could only make out his silhouette in the darkroom; he was slumped over and appeared to stare at the floor.

"George?" she said. "Oh, honey, it's really late. Why don't you come back to bed?" Her husband did not say anything but turned and crawled up to where his wife was. "Now get some rest so we can have another great day," Lydia said. She pulled up the blankets and they lay back down.

Lydia felt her husband toss and turn on the bed until he was comfortable. He spooned her, and she felt George's hot breath whispering across her skin. "Goodnight, Love," Lydia whispered back to her husband and snuggled into her place on the bed.

"Goodnight," a strange voice whispered back.

A wave of panic Panic flooded Lydia. She jumped from the bed in hysterics running for the door, a cold and rough hand grabbed her by the hair. "Let me go!" she screamed.

“Calm down, Lydia...it's me," the voice said.

Lydia paused for a moment—she knew that voice. “Richard?” she asked.

“Yes, it's me. Surprised?” the man asked sheepishly as he turned on the lights to the room.

“I didn't think you had the balls to actually come in our room,” Lydia said and turned to face the man. He was very tall, with long greasy hair that hung in his face, and wore a pair of overalls. “I thought you weren't going to be here until tomorrow.”

“Change of plans.”

“Well, when do you plan to take care of my husband?”

The tall man smiled. "I already did," he said as he picked up George's decapitated head from the floor. "Now, let's talk about payment."

THE LAST SUPPER

Dedicated to Ray Bradbury

WHEN I FIRST saw him walk into the diner, I honestly didn't put much thought into it. He was a fairly tall guy, maybe six foot or so and not too hard on the eyes, though the lines that started to develop on his face took away from his aura. He had long, thinning brown hair that was pulled back into a ponytail, wearing a khaki windbreaker, which appeared to be in need of a good washing. The other girls said that he had a dorky way about him. I assumed it was because of the metal-framed glasses he wore, but I couldn't make the same connection.

The man came to my diner every night. He sat in a booth at the far back, next to a large window. For some reason or another, I would volunteer to take his order, which would always be a New York steak and eggs done over-easy. While he waited for his food, the guy would sit there and stare out the window. I often wondered what he thought about and why he looked so alone and depressed.

I would find out exactly what was going on in his head soon enough, and in the end, I wished I hadn't.

I remember the night it all began. It was around eleven fifteen, and I just arrived to start my shift. Wilbur's Diner and Lodge wasn't a bad place to work, especially at night. We were across the street from a local hospital, so most of our customers were doctors, nurses, and other medical staff. The restaurant was pretty much empty other than our usual people from the hospital. As I went around the counter, I noticed him. He was at the the large window gazing out at the hospital. People would walk by, and he never took his eyes off the building across the street.

Tammy—the girl I took over for—asked me if I would serve this guy his food because she was late to get her kids from the babysitter. I told her it was no problem.

Not much later, our cook Tom told me that his food was ready—I didn't think too much about it as I picked up the plate and took it over to the customer.

"Here's your food, sir," I said as I placed the plate down in front of him. "Can I get you anything else?"

"No, thank you, this is fine," the man said with a soft smile. He looked up at me with misery-filled eyes; it appeared that he hadn't slept in some time.

As I walked back to the counter, I heard Sue—another waitress who worked the night-shift with me — snickering from the back room.

"What ya laughing about, Sue?" I asked her.

"It's the guy you just served. Tom said he thought he saw him on *Bum's Corner* the other night, and I told him I hope he doesn't try to pay with food stamps," Sue explained. I smirked at her and walked back out to the counter. I really didn't find that amusing—to make fun of someone's misfortune. I didn't give it any more thought and went back to work.

#

It was about forty-five minutes later when I heard that customer ask for his check.

"You go get his ticket Meg, and remind him he can't pay in food stamps," Sue laughed.

"Okay, no problem," I told her. I rang him up on the cash register and took the bill over to him. He remained fixed on the hospital as I walked up. "Here you go, sir. Now, will that be cash or credit?"

The man looked up at me with a thin smile. I hoped he hadn't overheard what Sue and Tom said about him being homeless. I didn't want any problems from my manager if he were to complain. My stomach knotted as he was about to speak. "Is cash all right, miss?"

"Yes. Yes, of course, it is, sir," I replied with a nod.

He pulled out a tattered black leather wallet, and when he opened it, my jaw almost crashed to the ground. It was *stuffed* with twenty-dollar bills; it had to be at least a couple of grand in there. He thumbed through the bills and handed me a ten. I told him that I'd be right back with his change.

"Na, you keep it, love. I don't need it where *I'm* going."

He again gave me a weak smile and left the diner. When I went back a few minutes later and began cleaning his table, I noticed a bill under a plate. When I lifted up the plate, I saw that the man left a fifty-dollar bill for my tip.

The rest of the night, I wondered what the man meant by *Where he's going,* and why he kept so much cash on him or left such a large tip for an eight dollar and fifty cent dinner. Besides, it's not like this was the safest place in the world, after all.

#

The next night when I came into work, I immediately noticed that the man was back and was seated in the same place he sat the night before. Sue, Tammy, and Tom were in the back again, but the conversation was about why a person with so much money looked the way this man did. Tom speculated that perhaps he was some type of wealthy hermit and was lonely, so he kept coming to the diner.

"What did he order tonight?" I asked.

"The same as last night—a New York steak and two eggs done over-easy," Tammy replied with a snicker. "Well, you or Sue can give him his food. It's time to blow this joint."

"I'll do it if you don't mind," I said. I wondered if there was another fifty-dollar tip in my future. I took the plate from Tom and walked it over to the guy who sat at the table. Once again, he glanced up at me with a weak smile. He had his glasses off, and I saw the dark circles under his eyes. The pain in his face was even more evident that night, not physical pain, but the kind that can only be felt through deep heartache.

"Good evening," the man said as he put his glasses back on.

"Hello, Mister..."

"Donald. But, please, you just can call me Don," he said.

"Hello, Don, here's your food," I said before I handed him his plate. "Is there anything else I can get for you?"

"No, thank you," Don replied. He took a bite of his eggs and turned his head back in the direction of the hospital.

I wasn't even back behind the counter yet, when Sue came out. "Well?" she asked.

"Well, what?" I asked.

"I saw you talking with him. What did he say?"

"He said that he didn't need anything else," I said to Sue. "Oh, and his name is Don."

"Well, you need to be careful with this guy. Money or no money, he's a weirdo," Tom said under his breath.

I gave them both a slight grin and went to do my usual duties.

"Hey? Where'd that guy go? Bastard left without paying," Sue informed us.

I looked over at her and shrugged my shoulders. How was I supposed to know—after all, I wasn't his keeper. "No clue," I said.

I walked over to his table. Don had neatly stacked his silverware and napkin on top of his empty plate. I lifted the plate, and there were two bills that time—a ten and a fifty. I heard Sue as she stomped her way toward me. I quickly slipped the larger bill into my pocket.

"He must have been in a hurry tonight because he left the money for the food on the table," I told her as I waved the ten-dollar bill at her.

#

Don continued to come in for his New York steak and eggs done over-easy meal. He remained relatively quiet, but every night left me a fifty-dollar tip. Over the next ten days, he gave me at least five hundred dollars in tips. That final night, as I was on my way into the diner, I decided to confront Don. I needed to understand what was up with this guy.

I got to work around the same time I did every night. When I got inside, I noticed Don wasn't there. In fact, the diner was completely empty. Perhaps it was because of the nasty winter rain outside. Tom and Sue were both over in the far booth; they watched a small television mounted in the corner. An old Orson Welles' movie was on—it was that *Rose Bud* one. I walked over to the booth and sat next to Sue. They were both so engrossed in the film; neither of them said a word.

"What are we watching?" I asked.

"Shhh! It's *Citizen Kane,*" Tom snapped; he never

took his eyes from the television.

"Oh. I thought it was that Rose Bud movie," I said. I hoped to strike up a conversation; I was never into old black and white movies.

"Child," Sue jumped in. "Do you even know what Rose Bud was?"

"Uh...No. I've never actually watched the movie," I replied. "I did a report on it when I was in school, but I just copied stuff from the Internet."

"Citizen Kane is a story about love and loss," Tom explained as he stared at the television. "Rose Bud was the name of a sled from Kane's childhood, which was about the only time he was really happy. It's an all-time classic."

"If you say so," I chuckled.

"I do—," Tom snipped before he was interrupted by the ring of the diner's doorbell.

"Finally, a customer," Sue said as he turned toward the entrance way. "Oh, look, Meg, it's your *friend*."

I turned and saw that it was indeed Don, but he appeared different that night. He was dressed in a *nice* black suit and tie with a leather windbreaker. His appearance was more like a power broker than a transient. Don walked over and sat at his usual table, then he immediately stared out the large window, but this time he smiled as he gazed off at the hospital.

"I'll go make his *damned* steak and eggs," Tom said in a huff.

I decided that it was a good time to confront Don about his *donations* to me before he started his meal. I got up and walked over to him, and as I approached the table, he glanced up at me with a warm smile.

"Good evening, Meg," he said in a soft tone.

"Hi, Don, you're late tonight," I joked.

"Yes, I spent a little extra time getting ready tonight," Don explained. "Please, have a seat. I can see that your associate has already started preparing my meal."

I seated myself in front of him and folded my hands on the table. I stared into his eyes, and while he continued to smile, I saw that the pain and sadness were still in his eyes.

"I have to ask you, Don. Why the fifty-dollar tip every night?" I asked. "I mean, I do appreciate it, but that's five hundred dollars you've given me in just a little over a week."

Don's smile grew wider. "I don't need it where *I'm* going," he explained.

"What do you mean? Are you *rich* or something?"

He let out a loud laugh. "Goodness, no, love," he replied as he continued to smile.

"Can you please explain, because I'm really confused," I said.

Don heaved a heavy sigh. He paused for a moment and stared deeply into my eyes. "You see, love, I used to work at that hospital across the street. I was a nurse there for a little over ten years. I was *let go* this past August," Don said and then paused for a moment. "I got caught up in a web of deception."

Don paused again. He looked back out the window at the hospital across the street before he began to speak again. "There was a rumor going around that I was sleeping with several co-workers, but they were just that—*rumors*. While I did have many friends there, it was always platonic; they were more of a second family to me."

He looked back toward me, and his smile turned into a frown. He lowered his head before he spoke again. "My boss called me into her office and confronted me about the rumors. I explained to her that they were nothing more than unfounded lies. She told me that she could make all of it go away and propositioned me. If I were to sleep with her, she'd make all of my problems disappear.

"I refused and tried to explain that I was a happily married man, and I would never break my vows. A week later, I was fired for reasons she made up...I don't even remember why now."

"I'm sorry to hear that, Don, I really am, but why give me so much money? Especially now that you have no job?" I asked. At this point, I was quite confused. I tried to make sense of what he had told me, but it only made the confusion worse.

"After I lost my job, you see, my wife took our kids and left. I have no clue where they could have gone, but nonetheless, they're gone," Don said. I noticed tears as they ran down his face. "Everything I had worked *so* hard for is gone."

"I'm *so* sorry, but—," I said before he interrupted me.

"I'm not rich at all. The money I have is from my last paycheck...I've made it last all these months, but since I'm going to *die* soon, I have no need for the rest of it." Don stopped again and pulled out his tattered wallet. He opened it and retrieved the money that remained inside. He handed me the cash, and his small smile returned. "Here. Take this; I won't need it after tonight."

“T-Thank you," I said while I thumbed through the cash. "But why won't you need it after tonight?"

“This is my last night alive,” he said as his smile grew wider. “I wasn't sure before when my end would come, but I am one hundred percent sure it will be tonight.”

Don laughed again, but this time it was more demented.

“You see...that's why I have ordered the same meal every night," he said. His eyes grew wilder with each second. "My mother used to make steak and eggs every Friday night when I was a child, and that has *always* been my favorite meal. And since I thought, I wouldn't live to see the next morning, I wanted my last meal to be my favorite."

“How come you're so certain tonight will be your final night on Earth?” I forced myself to ask.

“Because I'm going to end it with *this,*” Don replied as he pulled a Desert Eagle out from his windbreaker and placed it on the table.

Right then, Sue walked up to the table to deliver Don's meal to him. Once she saw the large handgun on the table, she began to scream hysterically.

“Omigod! Omigod! Please, please don't kill us," she cried out.

“Shhh... Shhh... Calm down, lady, I'm not going to

kill anyone," Don said as he stood up from the table.

"Omigod! Omigod! Omigod! I don't want to die," she continued.

Don said nothing when he picked up his weapon and placed a round into Sue's head without hesitation. The back of her skull exploded as blood and brain matter splattered on the table and wall behind her. It appeared that Sue tried to speak before she dropped lifelessly to the ground.

"You son of a bitch," Tom screamed as he charged toward Don with a butcher's knife held above his head. But he only made it halfway to us when Don fired another round and hit Tom dead center in the chest.

Before he turned back around, I snatched the cash from off the table and ran for the diner's door. I heard a loud gunshot from behind me, but I tried to reach the door before the bullet got me.

The bullet hit me underneath my left shoulder blade, and the force of the impact knocked me off my feet. I hit the ground with a hard *thud*, but I was still alive. Although the pain was unbearable, I tried to remain as still as possible. I felt my blood pool around my cheek and lips, but I stayed calm. I heard Don pick his plate off the table and walk toward me. My imagination ran wild: *Did he see me breathing?* I considered another attempt at the door, but the pain was too much for me to even move.

I played dead as he walked up to me, and I prepared for the worst. But instead, I watched him walk calmly walk away. I heard a fork as it scraped against a plate. I heard that a few more times before I listened to the diner's doorbell. I forced myself to look up. Don was nowhere in sight. I slowly got to my feet and staggered over to the door and glanced outside.

"He's gone," I cried. As I came back inside, I noticed a trashcan that was next to the doorway. An empty plate rested atop it with a ten-dollar bill placed in the center.

The End

RIDING SHOTGUN

BEN WATCHED THE white lines on Interstate 15 disappear rapidly beneath the wheels of his car. Traveling for hours in silence, he headed south toward Las Vegas on his way back home. Ben vowed over six years ago to never return home again unless it was for something essential, not being much of a family person.

A day ago, that a close friend from college was killed in a freak car accident. Ben planned to stay for a few days before he headed back to Aspen. The person responsible for his success was now dead, and he felt that it was his duty to honor Bobby's memory at the wake on Friday.

He received word of the accident on Tuesday afternoon, just as he finished up a lecture. His assistant handed him a small piece of paper as he stepped down from the podium. Since he was in the middle of a conversation with a student, Ben placed the small, folded piece of notepad paper in his pocket. A few hours later, he pulled a set of keys from his pocket, along with the folded note. Ben finally opened the paper. It read:

Mark called. He said that Bobby has been killed in a car accident.

Within a couple of hours, Benjamin was on the road, headed back to his hometown in California.

#

"Twelve forty-four in the morning," Ben said to himself as he looked at his wristwatch. "I should be in Barstow by at least three."

As he traveled down the darkened road, Reyes started to become uneasy with the spine-chilling silence. Ben tried to take his mind away from the eerie feeling and turned on the radio, thumbing through the stations trying to find one that would come in. Eventually, he came across a talk radio station; only a few miles farther up the road, the signal began to break up. Ben attempted to readjust the dial and then eventually gave up and turned off the radio.

No sooner did he start to feel better when the sensation of uneasiness returned. Ben attempted to talk himself out of it by blaming it on the darkness. Darkness was something that the young man never liked.

He searched his memories and questioned why being alone in the dark bothered him so much.

Then it came to him.

#

"Benjamin Reyes, come here this instant!" Ben's father demanded.

Young Ben did not like the tone in his father's voice; he knew that his dad had been drinking, and he also knew it was not safe to make him call twice. So, he replied quickly. "Coming, Poppa."

The boy peeked around a corner and saw his old man in the recliner waving a leather belt back and forth. Ben knew he was in some sort of trouble in his dad's eyes.

"Poppa, what did I do wrong?" Ben asked as he walked toward his father.

"Nothing, son, I just wanted you to come here," he replied with a slight smile.

The young child walked up to his father and faced him. Ben could smell the cheap whiskey that lingered on the old man's breath. The boy knew what was in store for him. He could see the anger now.

The drunken man quickly stood up from his chair without a word, grabbed the little boy by the hair, and started to violently strike Benjamin with the leather belt. The boy's cries echoed throughout the house, but no one came to his aide.

After the whipping, the older man dragged his son

to a closet, where he would lock him in for the rest of the day. The young boy would not say a word for hours on end. The only sound that came from the small child was a soft hum. He would hold his legs tightly and comfort himself against the surrounding darkness.

#

Once Benjamin reached the bottom of a long hill, a clunking sound came from under the hood of his vehicle. He could only get the car to go a few more miles up the road before the engine finally died. When the car came to a complete stop, Ben got out and walked around to the front.

As he opened the hood, thick dark smoke rose from the engine.

"Damnit," he muttered.

Ben pulled out his cell phone and got back inside the car. However, when he tried to use it, he noticed that the phone's screen flashed an 'out of service area' message. He got out of the car, slammed the driver's side door closed, and then walked away from the broken-down heap.

He traveled for hours up the road on foot but had an uneasy feeling that someone was following him. Ben increased his pace refusing to look back and see if someone was following him when he heard a strange noise. Ben's pace quickly escalated into a full-on sprint.

As he ran down the dimly lit highway, he heard a voice from the dark call out to him.

"Come with me," the voice called.

"No! Leave me alone!"

Even though he ran as fast as he could, Reyes still felt the heat of someone's breath on the back of his neck. "Come into the darkness with me," the voice said.

"Leave me the *fuck* alone!"

"We can taste your soul," the voice whispered, and Ben almost lost his balance.

until he felt something grab the back of his collar and begin to pull him down into a pool of darkness.

"*Noooooooooo!*" Ben screamed.

Once he came to his senses, Ben found that he stood in the center of a small, rundown town as the young man looked around, he noticed a sign that read, 'Welcome to Barstow.' But he wondered how that could be possible, since the last he remembered, he was still a few miles from the outskirts of town.

"What the *hell* is going on here?" he asked himself trying to catch his breath. Ben was shaking uncontrollably, so he lowered himself to the curb regrouping his thoughts. He wiped the sweat from his forehead and let out a shaky sigh.

#

As the young Benjamin sat alone inside the dark closet, he continued to hold himself tight and rock back and forth. As he soothed his fear, Ben hummed to himself softly, while evil snickers were heard all around him.

His soft hum was interrupted when something called the child's name from the darkness.

"Benjamin…Benjamin…We know you are there; we can smell your soul."

He replayed his little tune, now a bit louder, while he rocked with more force. He felt the terror that was in the tiny room with him. Ben closed his eyes tightly and tried to act as if he did not hear the voices. But they still called out to him.

"Why do you ignore us, Benny? We only want to play with you. Come over to us, and we'll play a fun game."

"Leave me alone—Please." the boy pleaded.

"Come on, it will be fun."

"Please…I'm scared…just leave me alone."

"There is nothing to be afraid of," the voice assured him. "Come to us, and we'll take good care of you."

"I said, go away, *please!*" Ben screamed.

Then he felt cold hands with long fingers, clutch his shoulders, and hot breath heated the back of his neck. "Benny, tell me…do you know what Hell is?" the voice asked.

#

"Hey, buddy, are you all right?" someone asked, and Ben opened his eyes.

A bright light was flashed in his eyes as he looked up. He raised his hand to block the glare from his face, and Ben could see that the light came from a police cruiser.

"Yeah…yeah, I'm all right. I just got a little light-headed, so I sat down for a moment," Ben replied.

The officer turned off the light, and Ben was able to see again. Not wholly sure whether Ben was a threat or not, the cop slowly made his way over to him. He stopped a few steps away.

"So, what are you doing out here in the middle of the night?" the officer asked.

"My car broke down a few miles back, so I was walking into town looking for a phone to call for a ride to come and pick me up."

"There's one about three blocks down," the cop said and then went back to his car. "Oh, and if I were you, I would stay in the light."

"W-what?" Ben asked.

But the officer did not answer as he closed his door and abruptly drove away. That comment caused Ben to feel even more uneasy about his current situation. He got back to his feet with a heavy sigh and slowly started in the direction of the nearest phone.

As he traveled along the dimly lit sidewalk, Ben could once again feel the *evil* that resided in the darkness. Just when his nerve was about to give, there it was—the phone booth only a few steps away, but that did not stop the laughter that came from the beasts that waited for him.

"Benjamin, come out and play," they called to him.

"Go away!" he said.

"Benjamin, why won't you share your *delicious* soul," a voice growled.

With one last step, he entered the safe confines of the phone booth. Ben stood there for a moment in relief and could feel warmth emanate from the small light of the booth that was above him.

He knew now that everything was going to be all right as he placed a call to Mark.

#

After a twenty-minute wait, Mark pulled up to find that his friend Ben still waiting for him in the phone booth. When he honked his horn, Ben dashed from the stall and into the waiting car.

“Benny! How are you doing, buddy?” Mark asked.

“I'm doing okay, I guess. I'm glad you're here, though," Ben replied. They pulled away from the booth, and no one said anything else until they turned back onto the Interstate. "I can't believe Bobby died," Ben said. "He was so young and full of life. How could something like that happen to a guy like him?"

“Yeah, he was a good guy, but let's not think about that right now. This is just like old times, isn't it? I'm here, you're here riding shotgun—what could be better?” Mark asked as he drove off into the surrounding darkness.

#

“That was a beautiful service Mrs. Hackmen. I'm sure Mark would have been pleased,” one of the mourners said.

“Thank you, Bobby. But what happened to your friend, Benjamin? Mark used to speak so highly of him.”

"I don't know Mrs. Hackmen," Bobby said. "I called and left a message with his assistant, but he never called me back. I guess he was just too busy to come."

The End

Call of the Blackbird

Dedicated to Edgar Allan Poe

SEPTEMBER 22, 1910

Today I saw them perched high in a willow tree. They watched as we put my dear Aunt Matilda to rest. Though she was ninety-two years old, her death was unexpected, and yet the physicians claimed it was due to natural causes. But I knew better; her passing was no cause of nature, but an act of *murder,* and the killer's identity I knew all too well.

Those demons were in the tree; though they watched from high above, I heard laughter from their perfect crime. But I knew of their secret, although everyone dismissed it as the senile ramblings of an old man. I knew that the crows were messengers of death, and they were here to put my family and me six feet under.

As I was wheeled away from the gravesite, I

watched as those monstrous creatures ascend back into the sky and headed home—my home.

September 25, 1910

The house had been quiet for a few days now; everyone is still in mourning my dear aunt's death. I noted that there appeared to be more blackbirds that morning. Usually, there were half a dozen or so that flocked around the estate, but I saw them out the corner window when I was rolled into the sitting room.

Two or three *dozen* of those damned birds. The trees had lost their green hue from the sheer number of harbiger's of doom that sat on each branch as if every leaf on the tree had died and turned black as a winter's night.

I watched them for hours as they plotted their next victim; if only I knew who it was… I could protect them, or at best, warn them of their coming misfortune.

September 26, 1910

I was unable to sleep last night. The blackbirds cawed until sunrise; I knew it was a warning to their next victim. They would strike soon and take the life of another dear family member, but who—would it be my own life they would come for next?

I found that I now feared for my life. Though three decades past my prime, I was not ready to enter the afterlife, which awaited me. I thought of my damned luck—Polio took my legs, and *now* would the blackbirds take the rest?

I will end this entry early; perhaps I will find slumber in the daylight and be safe from an attack of those wicked beasts that sit outside my home and wait —wait to take their next soul to the underworld.

September 30, 1910

Today I learned that my dear brother Wilbur was quite ill. He had complained of his chest burning for a few days now, and this morning he was too weak to get out of bed and continued to struggle for breath. Were the blackbirds responsible for this? Did they come amid the night and hurt my dear brother?

From that, I decided today that I would no longer sleep at night, but instead during the day to be safe from the evil meddling of the killer birds, for I am confident now that they strike at night when we are all most vulnerable.

October 1, 1910

I was told this evening when I awoke that my brother Wilbur appeared to be doing much better and that he was now able to speak and appeared to be on a fast road to recovery. In fact, his nurse said that she would be going home for the evening and returning in the morning since he no longer needed twenty-four-hour care.

Finally, a bit of good is brought into this household!

October 2, 1910

Poor Wilbur died this morning. His nurse found him blue and lifeless. I think she seeing the pattern that I had been seeing for the last few weeks. Now I fear for the woman's safety as well as my own. I overheard her say Wibur appeared to have suffocated, but his lungs sounded clear just last night when she left. It was those damned birds! Those monsters took my dear aunt's life and now—now my poor beloved brother's, as well!

October 5, 1910

As we all prepared for my beloved brother's burial services, I was quite mortified to see that there was a flock of blackbirds sitting on every ledge of our house. Several cawed, but I heard laughter for yet another perfect murder.

I watched them follow us to the graveyard; perching in the same tree they were in on the day we buried my dear Aunt Matilda. A gentle breeze crossed the cemetery as the minister began his eulogy. A smell wafted past us, which was a combination of freshly cut grass…and death.

After the services, a few of those damn birds remained to watch my poor brother's body be returned to the Earth. It turned out to be something that would haunt me for the rest of my years. One of the undertaker's ropes snapped causing the other men to lose balance, and they dropped the wooden coffin to the ground. Upon impact, the container burst open, and my brother's lifeless body fell into the grave.

It was not so much the sight of his body which disturbed me… it was his face—frozen in time at the very moment he passed over to the other side. His mouth hung open in fear, and his brow remained in the position of utter fright. I witnessed the devil's handy work that day and shuddered at what horrid death those monsters had in store for me.

October 13, 1910

This morning, I read in the paper that the police found the young and beautiful nurse, Abigail, dead in front of her house. The article said she was strangled to death, but what the reporter found odd was that her mouth was crammed full of *black* feathers. The author may not have understood, but I did, completely. The young nurse must have brought too much attention to herself about my poor brother's untimely death. And those damned birds must have felt her knowledge was too much of a threat for her to continue to live.

She was such a lovely and beautiful creature, a gentle caregiver to the ill. She did not deserve a vicious death... I hope those blackbirds rot in hell for all they have done.

October 17, 1910

I was unable to sleep last at all yesterday. A dozen or so blackbirds sat at my ledge and, with their beaks, tapped the window ever so lightly. For hours at a time, all I heard was, Tick...Tick...Tick...

The others in the house glared at me as if I was insane, as if somehow, they heard nothing from the blackbirds! They continued on throughout the night. When my nerves were their weakest point, the flock flew away from my window, each cawing in mockery at my emotional torment.

October 18, 1910

I am happy to report that I was allowed by those demonic creatures to sleep last night. Though my mind wanted to wander as to what they were up to, my frail old body demanded rest, and before I knew what had happened, I woke up with a rooster's crow.

I must admit that I feel rather rejuvenated; perhaps I will travel out to the courtyard today and greet the sun.

October 21, 1910

I just learned that Percy died today. Too upset to elaborate; he was so young—your senile old uncle will remember you, child.

October 22, 1910

I am ready to talk about what happened yesterday. My young nephew Percy died in a plowing accident; he was preparing the harvest when his horse was spooked, flipped the plow on top of the boy, and one of the long blades came loose, impaling him.

I wheeled myself off to the site of the accident. As I expected, I found several scattered black feathers about the area. It appears that the blackbirds have claimed yet another life for their dark master.

October 23, 1910

Jarvis, the estate's caretaker, left today. I begged him not to leave, but he accused me of the murders! I tried to explain that it was, the blackbirds that hung overhead, but he scoffed at me and said I was mad.

Those demon birds have turned what little remains of my family against me, and now I am all alone and undoubtedly, the final victim.

I must prepare myself for the final battle, for I refuse to be another soul taken for the devil's amusement.

October 29, 1910

It had been six days since I was left alone with the blackbirds, and though they have not yet attacked, I saw them out my window...flying and rallying the others for our final encounter. The sun is high overhead, and I feel that this is the safest time to sleep.

Before I close for the day, I wanted to let you know of my little trap I set this morning at sunrise. I placed a small surprise underneath a willow tree in the courtyard. If all goes according to plan, I will dine on blackbird pie for supper.

October 30, 1910

When I woke up today, I realized I had overslept. The morning's sun had just ascended into the sky. For a moment, I wondered why the blackbirds didn't come for me while I was asleep. Then I realized why: they themselves must have had been in mourning. I pulled myself onto the wheelchair and rolled outside as fast as I could.

I wheeled myself to the willow tree in the courtyard, and there one of the beasts hung. It had fallen for the trap. Moving closer to the dead bird I untied it from the tree and placed it in my lap and began to wheel myself back inside the house as quickly as possible. I was afraid that the monster would return to life and take its vengeance on me.

I went into the kitchen and placed the bird on the counter and began to pluck the feathers from its body until the bird was clean. I sat there for a moment as I admired my handy work, and then to my surprise, the beast began to move. I grabbed a large knife and severed the creature's head. Even decapitated, it continued to twitch as blood freely flowed from its neck. It took several moments before the bird finally lied still. I spent the next hour or so preparing my *blackbird* pie, and not long after, I had it in the oven.

At supper, I placed the pie on the table and served myself a helping. As I was about to take the first bite, I heard them outside the window. Some tapped on the glass, while others cawed. I let out a laugh at those monsters. "I have victory tonight," I told them and then took a bite filled with pleasure.

The birds remained at the window for the duration of my meal. Finally, filled with contempt toward my unwanted dinner guests, I took the final bite of the blackbird pie. I stared at them as I slowly chewed the morsel. The creatures were silent as they watched me finish feasting on their fallen comrade.

After dinner, I wheeled myself back to my room. I watched out of the corner of my eye as the beasts followed along from outside. Once I entered my room, I rolled up to the window and saw one blackbird that sat on the ledge. We stared at each other for some time before the bird squawked and bowed its head in defeat. I told the little demon that I accepted his surrender and to leave in peace. I swore it when he appeared to smile at me and then flew away into the night.

That night, I slept soundly, as I knew I was victorious against the monstrous blackbirds.

October 31, 1910

I was awakened around three; hearing the call of a blackbird, but when I sat up in bed and glanced toward the window, there was no one there. I lied back down and tried to go back to sleep, but I heard it again when I closed my eyes. At first, I ignored it, but the bird continued to cry out. I screamed out for it to leave that I had won, and the fight was over.

It stopped momentarily until I heard the monster in my ear. It cawed as loud as the beast could. I quickly jumped and attempted to catch the bird because I knew it was somehow inside the house with me and was now next to me. But when I turned toward the blackbird, there was nothing there. I sat in my bed and glancing around the room, but there was nothing.

Then, I heard the caw once more. It was again in my ear, but how could that have been? My question was answered when my stomach cramped and turned. I heard the beast as it laughed at me from inside my body. Somehow, the little demon reassembled itself inside me and wanted out.

The laughter grew louder by the second, and at that moment, I knew what had to be done. I pulled myself onto the wheelchair and rolled quickly through the house until I found myself in the kitchen. I needed to remove the blackbird from inside me and kill it once and for all. I wheeled over to where our knives were kept and studied each instrument carefully.

Eventually, I decided on the paring knife. I knew the blade was small enough to not hurt me, and I could extract the animal with ease. I placed the knife on the surface of my stomach, and as the creature continued its insane laughter, I plunged the small, sharp steel blade into my belly.

Blood ran from my stomach as I continued to cut and moved the blade along my flesh. Tears flowed down my face as I cut deeper, but I refused to give the bird the satisfaction of hearing me cry out in pain, so I remained silent. Once I had a big enough of a hole opened, I slid my finger inside to retrieve the monster, but then I realized that the bird was not only inside me, but it was inside my *stomach*.

I felt it as it moved around inside me, and I knew what I had to do to free myself of the little demon. I plunged my hand inside the wound, and against my best efforts not to, I screamed out in unfathomable pain. I felt the bird as it moved around inside my stomach and I grabbed and pulled the organ from my body.

I threw the bag made of skin on the counter and watched in horror as it twitched around. I needed to move quickly, as I felt warm blood gush from me. I saw the large blade I used earlier to prepare the pie and snatched it up. In a blind frenzy, I begin to hack down at the beast that was trapped inside my stomach. Within mere moments, I had chopped the bird into small pieces.

As I sat there, I knew I would no longer hear the call

of a blackbird.

#

Excerpt from the Ragsdale Gazette.

Police were called to Knolls Convalescent Home. A small, local, eight-bed facility, where they were horrified to find the home's elderly residents and one nurse had been murdered. Decomposing bodies were found in several different bedrooms. The complex was empty of other staff, and officials stated that another dead body was found in the kitchen area.

Jasper O'Neil, 86, was found dead in his wheelchair, which was located in the kitchen. Seemingly was the murderer's final victim. His stomach viciously removed from his body and chopped into fine slices on a nearby counter. Close to this grotesque display on the counter was a blood-splattered journal that Mr. O'Neil may have been writing in prior to his murder.

Anyone with information regarding these crimes should contact the Ragsdale Police Department.

LOLA'S SPECIAL GIFT

IT WAS EARLY morning when Henry Zeltman walked into his house. He just finished a shift at the local paper mill and was ready to retire for the day. His bones popped in protest as he sat down in his favorite recliner. Zeltman had worked at the paper mill for almost fifteen years. He was well aware that he was overworked and underpaid in this profession, but it was an honest living, which mattered most to him. Even so, that sort of work began to take a toll on him not only physically but mentally as well.

Henry was forty-three years old, and he never thought in a million years that he would still be employed at the paper mill at this age. Zeltman always dreamed of being a Hollywood actor. When he was in his twenties and thirties, all his friends used to tell him he was made for movies; Henry was six foot three, well built, with blond hair and blue eyes. But that was then.

Now Zeltman was a balding, blue-eyed man who stood with a slight stoop after being injured in an accident at the paper mill some years ago. He knew his youthful dreams were far long gone, but every now and again, Henry would lose himself in the world of 'what if.'

Henry saw clearly a life of fame, fortune, large mansions, and beautiful women, traveling the globe, and being the star of countless feature films. Zeltman would sit in his chair, lost in this fantasy until he was fast asleep.

#

"Henry!"

"W-what?" Henry responded, as he quickly sat up straight in his recliner to find that his wife of twenty years, Lola, stood in front of him. She held a plate of food, and an unopened beer.

"Hurry up and wake your ass up! My head is killing me!" Lola exclaimed. She had frequent headaches for reasons unknown, which limited her ability to do pretty much anything.

"Okay, I'm awake," Henry murmured. "What did you ma--"

Lola interrupted him as she tossed the plate into Henry's lap. "Here, your lazy ass slept over, so I made hot dogs," she snapped.

Zeltman grinned, but only to himself. This wasn't quite what he had planned for dinner, but it was a welcome break from having to cook. Henry looked up at his wife and forced a wide smile. "Thank you, love."

"Yeah, whatever," Lola spat as she walked away.

Zeltman sighed heavily. He stared down at the plate in front of him and plucked the sausage up out of the bun. "Huh, no mustard," he murmured.

"Henry!"

"Coming," Zeltman said after another heavy sigh. He got up from the recliner and stumbled into the kitchen and over to the refrigerator. Henry put his plate inside, but before he could even close the door, she called again.

"HENRY!"

"For god sakes," Henry mumbled to himself. He walked down the hallway to a back bedroom. There Zeltman found his wife in bed with the T.V. on. "What do you need, hun?"

"Took you long enough!" Lola hissed. "Did I interrupt something? Were you out spanking the monkey while you were thinking of some skinny bitch?"

"No, I was trying to eat my dinner before I head off to work," Henry replied. "So, what do you want, babe?"

"Babe, my ass," she sneered. "You're probably not even going to work; you're probably going out to fuck some hottie. So, what's her na--"

"What do you want? I have to get ready."

"Take my plate. I'm all done."

"Good lord," Zeltman said. He took the plate and walked out of the room before she could think of anything else to say.

#

Less than an hour later, Henry was in his car and on his way to the paper mill. He always enjoyed the hour-long drive that it took to get there. It was his opportunity to clear his thoughts and be ready to work by the time he got to work at eleven o'clock.

The warm night air rushed into Zeltman's old Buick as he raced down the freeway. His favorite song, *Don't fear the Reaper,* blared from the rear speakers. *It was the song of my teen years,* Henry thought to himself each time it came on the radio. It was during those years he could say he was totally free. Shortly thereafter, Henry met Lola, and while they dated six years before the two got married, things remained unchanged since their 'I do's.'

After the song ended, there was a brief silence. *The D.J. must be off his game tonight,* Zeltman thought. Henry jumped as the radio station came back on the air.

96.6 DMON radio

There were another few moments of silence before the sound again came from the back speakers.

Are you tired of your miserable life?

"You have no clue, Mister," Henry replied back to the man on the radio.

Well, you could always put a gun in your mouth and blow your God-forsaken brains out.

"Do what? I'm surprised they let him say that on the radio."

But, you don't have the balls to pull the trigger, do you—you chicken shit?

"Am I hearing this, right?" Zeltman asked himself.

Well, my friend, then you are in luck. C'mon down to Wonderland Emporium, where for a reasonable price, we can make all your dreams come true!

"Yeah, right," Henry scoffed. He flipped through the stations until he came across Led Zeppelin and hummed along with them until he reached the paper mill.

#

It was just ten more minutes until Henry arrived at the parking lot. His thoughts traveled back to his wife's comments about going to see another woman as he got out of the old Buick. *Yeah, I wish,* Zeltman thought to himself. As he walked into the mill, he was greeted by several co-workers. Henry was a well-respected person at work. After many years of service to the company, Zeltman got the nickname "Handyman Henry" because he could troubleshoot just about any problem that might arise within the mill. Many of his co-workers frequently asked him why he was not a supervisor after all those years. With a fake smile, Henry's reply was always the same and then shrug his shoulders, but the truth was the current supervisor was the nephew of the majority shareholder of the mill. He knew that as long as the nephew wanted the job, Henry was S.O.L.

Zeltman took his place at his workstation. He was a plant engineer, and his job was to click a button every thirty seconds to ensure that heat did not over-dry or burn the fresh roll of newly made paper. Henry had done this job for so long he was able to do other tasks, like read the newspaper or watch television, keeping in perfect sync with the paper production line.

Tonight, he watched his favorite show; it was about a down on his luck shoe salesman, his money-hungry wife, and their two pathetic children. Zeltman did not find the series all that funny, but at least there was somebody whose life was worse than his; even if it was fictional, he could still laugh at that.

The T.V. show cut to a commercial, and Henry turned his attention back to the production line. Everything looked perfect. At least he could still take pride in how well he did his job. As Zeltman pushed down on the button, his top shirt pocket buzzed.

"Damn it," Henry said, aware of who the text was from even before he pulled the phone out of his pocket. Zeltman flipped the top back on his phone and saw the text message. It read:

'Can U call me?'

Henry chuckled to himself as he replied: 'I'm on the line; I don't get a break until one.'

Before Henry was able to put the phone back into his pocket, it buzzed once again. Zeltman held the device in his hand for a moment before he opened it; he already knew it would be a stinging response from his wife, Lola. Finally, he flipped back open the phone, and the message inside read:

'Okay, nice that your drinking buddies can talk to you all day while they're at work! I will email you 'cause that's the way you like to talk anymore!'

Zeltman was about to engage in a texting battle with his wife, but someone's shout made him snap his head up.

"*Shit!* Henry!"

Henry looked and saw his supervisor, who pointed toward the heater. "Hurry your ass up and hit the button before it burns!" he snapped.

Zeltman slammed his hand down on the button and watched, as well as prayed, as the paper rolled out of the heater.

"Please. Please, oh, please, don't be burnt," Henry said as the paper began to roll out from under the heater. His stomach knotted when he saw the sheet as it rolled into open sight. As Henry continued to click the button, he stood up and saw the paper—it was a fresh white strand of fifty-pound stock.

"Thank god," he sighed.

"You're lucky, Zeltman," the supervisor said. "Another screw up like that, and your ass is mine!"

"Y-yes, sir. I-I'm sorry, sir, it won't happen again." Zeltman muttered

"Now get back to work," the supervisor told him.

Henry watched the supervisor as he walked back into his office and slammed the door. Zeltman hung his head in humiliation while an image of a physical confrontation between the two of them sped through his mind. Henry knew that even though he had ten years on the supervisor, an altercation would end badly for the younger man. As Henry sat there buried in his thoughts, he listened to the television for any signs that his favorite show came back on. He hoped to get lost in the program and be able to laugh at someone else's misfortune other than his own, but instead, a familiar voice from earlier came out of the T.V. set.

ARE YOU TIRED OF YOUR MISERABLE LIFE?

"Huh, you again, eh?" Henry huffed under his breath.

DO YOU WORK FOR SOME SNOT-NOSED TWIT, WHO YOU'D LOVE TO TAKE OUT BACK?

Henry responded with a soft laugh.

YOU COULD WALK RIGHT INTO HIS OFFICE AND BEAT THE LITTLE BASTARD'S A.S.S.

"That's an idea, bu--"

BUT, YOU DON'T HAVE THE BALLS TO DO THAT, DO YOU? – YOU CHICKENSHIT.

"I lost my spine a long time ago, mister," Zeltman said, and a wave of self-pity flooded over him.

WELL, MY FRIEND, THEN YOU ARE IN LUCK. C'MON DOWN TO WONDERLAND EMPORIUM, WHERE FOR A REASONABLE PRICE WE CAN MAKE ALL YOUR DREAMS COME TRUE.

Henry laughed at himself for even listening to that stupid commercial. He turned to the man who sat to his left. "Steve, can you cover me?" Henry asked. "I really need a cigarette."

#

Henry glanced up at a clock that hung on the wall near his station and broke a thankful smile when he saw it was thirteen minutes until seven o'clock. Eight-hour shifts had become quite difficult for him ever since he turned forty, but they got worse when he transferred to nights three years ago. Zeltman caught a glimpse of the supervisor as he left his office, and Henry's stomach turned when he noticed that the boss walked directly toward him. Paranoid thoughts raced through his head, and by the time the younger man stood in front of him, Henry felt faint. But something was not right; the supervisor wore a smile, although Henry knew it was as phony as the guy's degree that hung in his office.

"What do you want from me, Ray?"

The supervisor stepped back and assessed Henry for a moment, then his fake smile grew even more prominent. "I know tonight is your day off," Ray said, "but I need you to work over an hour or two."

"Two hours of Double Time?" Zeltman asked.

"Yes, sir," Ray replied.

"Are you working over as well?"

"Uh, no… no, they don't need me to stay over."

Henry cracked a smile of his own. "Tell your uncle I'll stay over."

#

Zeltman watched as the clock moved to twelve minutes to nine. He hadn't worked a ten-hour shift in years, and all he could think about was dozing off in his comfortable recliner when he got home.

Henry heard the 'click' of the extended hand as it

moved up one more minute, and then his cell phone buzzed in his shirt pocket. Instantly, Zeltman felt nauseated, as the vibration was a late reminder to text his wife and let her know he was working overtime. He sighed loudly as he flipped open the phone. The text read:

'Where are ya at?'

Zeltman knew whatever his response was, it wouldn't be the right one, so he texted back:

'Work. I leave at nine.'

Henry didn't even close his phone. He already knew she would have a reply to it before he finished. It didn't take long; the phone buzzed. Zeltman shook his head as he read:

'You fucking suck the mill's dick!'

Before Henry could reply, it buzzed again and said:

'You fucking faggot!'

With that, Zeltman closed his phone, and though it buzzed several more times, he put it back into his shirt pocket and refused to read any further messages.

#

It was a few minutes after ten in the morning when Henry walked into his house. Tired and weary, he staggered over to his recliner and collapsed into it. The soft exterior welcomed his body, and at that single moment in time, all Henry wanted was to go to sleep.

"HENRY!" Lola shouted from the back of the house.

Zeltman's blood-shot eyes opened, and a blanket of frustration covered him. Henry felt tears as they streamed down his face, and his wife continued to call out his name.

"HENRY! ARE YOU HERE YET?"

Henry pulled himself from his recliner and limped down to the bedroom. When Zeltman walked into the room, he saw his wife on the bed, and she held a washcloth over her eyes. He stumbled over next to her and sat down on the bed. "What do you need, love?" Henry asked softly.

"I need my fucking pills, where are they?" Lola exclaimed. She looked out from under the cloth to see if Henry held any bottle in his hand, but there was nothing. "Well, where they at?"

"I-I, I didn't realize that I was supposed to get them for you," Zeltman mumbled.

"What? Whatever!" Lola spat. "If you'd read your text messages instead of playing with yourself, you'd have known!"

Without a word, Henry stood up and exited the room.

Lola yelled at his back. "Now, where ya going?"

Zeltman clearly heard her but had nothing left to say to her. Instead, he walked out the front door and headed for his car. Once inside, the speakers rang out in the back:

ARE YOU TIRED OF YOUR MISERABLE LIFE?

"Shut the hell up already!" Henry screamed and turned off the radio. He sat in the driveway for a few moments to collect himself. He was tired and frustrated, but he had to take care of his wife and eventually backed out to pick up her medication.

#

It was later that evening when Henry woke up in his recliner. The living room was dark and comfortable. For the first time in months, Zeltman got to wake up on his own. *Small blessings,* he thought to himself. Henry glanced down at his watch and saw it was almost eight at night; it was time for his favorite sports program. He had been a fan of mixed martial arts for many years before it became popular, and it was an extra treat that came on public television once a week.

Henry had a few minutes before the show began, so he jumped up and ran to the fridge. Zeltman pulled out his last Boston Lager and then headed back into the living room. He sat down in his recliner while he slowly sipped his frothy cold beverage and readied himself for a couple hours of old -fashioned pugilism.

"Henry!"

The unexpected shout caused Zeltman to jump, and the lager he held tipped over into his lap. "Great. Just great."

Henry got up and walked into the bedroom. "What?"

"You need to take the trash out, and we're out of drinks; you need to go to the store too," Lola said. She paused for a moment while she examined his wet pants. "What did you do to yourself?"

"I split my lager," Zeltman sniped.

"Okay, sure, don't tell me then. What are you doing?"

"I'm watching the fights. Why?"

"Why are you watching that gay ass show? It's just a bunch of guys who run around in their boxers…you like that shit, don't you?" Lola rumbled.

"Yeah, I enjoy watching the fight," Henry replied and knew that his wife must be bored, so she was looking for a fight.

"See, I told you that you were a fag. You just prove it by you watching that shit."

Zeltman felt the anger cascade over him; he was tired of the constant insults and belittling. But, he also knew that was precisely what Lola wanted, and Henry didn't have anything in him for a confrontation.

"What did you want, by the way?" Henry asked after a few moments of self-meditation.

"Oh, you need to mow the lawn. It's overgrown, and I don't want people to think we're slobs," Lola sniped.

Zeltman snickered to himself as he walked away.

"What's so funny?" Lola snapped.

Henry paused and looked over his shoulder. "Do you have any clue what time of day it is?" he asked. "It's already dark outside. I'll do it tomorrow."

"Sure, you will."

Henry exited the room and ignored what his wife said. He walked back to the recliner. "Ah, much better," Zeltman noted to himself as he sat back down. "Much better."

Zeltman tried to focus on the television, but he heard his wife in the back of the room as she swore and carried on about God knows what. Henry thought about closing her door when a familiar voice came from the T.V.:

ARE YOU TIRED OF YOUR MISERABLE LIFE?

"Really, these commercials have great timing," Henry said. "Yeah, yeah, I am tired."

WELL, YOU COULD ALWAYS JUST PACK YOUR BAGS AND GET THE HELL OUT OF THERE.

"Yeah, I could."

BUT YOU'RE NOT MAN ENOUGH TO STAND UP FOR YOURSELF, ARE YOU?

"No. No, I'm not," Zeltman said with a regretful sigh.

WELL, MY FRIEND, THEN YOU ARE IN LUCK! C'MON DOWN TO WONDERLAND EMPORIUM, WHERE FOR A REASONABLE PRICE WE CANMAKE ALL YOUR DREAMS COME TRUE!

"Do you have a payment plan?" Henry asked sarcastically and then took a long drink that finished off the rest of his lager.

BUT WAIT! IF YOU CALL NOW OR STOP BY THE STORE IN THE NEXT THIRTY MINUTES, WE WILL SET YOU UP WITH A FIRST COME FIRST SERVE PAYMENT PLAN.

"Really?"

YEAH, REALLY, SO COME ON DOWN!

#

Zeltman told Lola he was headed to the store to get a few things but ended up in front of the Wonderland Emporium. The building was huge; it would dwarf a massive aircraft hangar. It was painted a fresh white and over the entranceway hung an enormous lighted sign that read: WONDERLAND EMPORIUM.

"I must be crazy to be here," Henry said to himself while he stood near the doorway.

"Crazy or desperate, my friend," a voice from behind him said. Zeltman turned and saw a tall, older man. He was slender and tall, wearing a black suit and tie with a fedora hat, matching the rest of his outfit.

"Who are you?" Zeltman asked.

"I'm the owner and manager of this beautiful store before you," the man said proudly. "I remember when I first started out, and it was just a simple Antique Shop."

"So, you really have products that could make my life better?"

"Better?" The man laughed and walked toward Zeltman. "Why, my friend, we have a product here that will allow you to have the life you've always wanted!"

"What's your name again?" Henry asked now that the older man stood right in front of him.

"I didn't give it friend, but my friends call me Luci, with an 'I.' So, do you want to walk inside and let me show you the things that will change your life forever?" Luci asked.

"Okay, lead the way," Henry replied.

"Oh, and don't forget, we offer a money-back guarantee," the old man said as he and Henry walked into the building.

#

Less than an hour later, Henry returned home. The house was dark and quiet. He sauntered to the back of the house and saw Lola fast asleep. Zeltman couldn't help but break a smile. *Peace and quiet,* Henry thought, feeling his way through the darkness until he came upon his recliner. After he seated himself, he found the remote control and clicked on the television. The large screen illuminated the small living room just enough for Henry to see the little box which he held in his right hand.

The box was made of wood with tiny intricate carvings of a solar system, complete with several moons and stars wrapped around the container. It was trimmed in a highly polished gold leaf, and the lid was carved in the shape of a pyramid reminding Zeltman of something that came out of Egypt. Where the pyramid came together, there was a small golden sun. The bottom was made from wood and gold. Zeltman was surprised how light the container was, because it was only the size of an apple. Staring at the object he held in his hands until he became lost in his own daydreams—dreams of a life of fame and fortune. Then Zeltman quickly returned to his unkind reality as he heard a shout from behind him.

"Henry!"

Zeltman turned and saw his wife behind him, and she appeared to be livid for reasons known only to her. She stomped around the chair until she faced him. "I've been calling you, fucker!" she snapped.

"I'm... I'm sorry. I didn't hear you. I thought you

were asleep," Zeltman muttered to his wife.

"I was until this headache came on," Lola replied. There was a brief moment of silence as the two looked at each other. Lola seemed like an animal about to strike her prey, while Henry looked like the helpless creature that saw the predator and was too frightened to move.

"Do...do you...want me to go to the store and get you something?" Henry babbled.

"What's the use? Nothing fucking works!" Lola barked. Before she could walk away, Lola noticed the small box Henry held. "What's that?" she demanded, and before Zeltman could answer, Lola reached down and ripped the container from his hands.

Lola looked the box over quickly and then again more slowly. "It's gorgeous..." she said softly.

Zeltman did not respond—he was too stunned. Henry could not remember the last time she spoke softly to him, about anything.

"Is this for one of your bitches at work?" she snapped,; all softness once again gone from her voice.

Henry managed a weak smile. "It's for you, love," he said sheepishly.

"Oh, really? Why?" she demanded, suspicious as always.

"Just because I thought of you when I saw it," Zeltman answered. "Open it and see what's inside."

Without hesitation, Lola removed the top and excitedly looked down into the box. Instantly her expression changed to confusion, and she looked up at Henry with pure hatred. "Is this a fucking joke?"

"What do you mean?" Zeltman asked.

"I mean, it's fucking *empty!*" Lola shouted and still held the empty box close to her face. "It wasn't for me, was it? You were gonna give it to one of those whores, weren't y—"

Lola's tirade was cut short as dozens of tiny, skeletal hands reached out of the box and grabbed onto her face. She let out a scream and tried to drop the container, but it was too late; the hands had their bone-like fingers buried deep into her flesh.

Lola collapsed to the floor as she continued to scream in pain and fear. The tiny hands now began to retract back into the box, and as they did so, they pulled her face closer to the opening. Lola tried to stop them as she attempted to hold the container at a distance, but within moments the box was right up next to her face. She continued to scream, now in total panic. Lola's facial bones cracked and snapped as her head was forced into the small box, but at least her screams finally stopped. Her body contorted, then bent and folded in on itself. She was pulled further inside until, her entire body had been drawn entirely into the box and disappeared.

Amazed and horrified by what he just witnessed, Henry simply sat there for a full minute staring at the box. When the dazed husband came to his senses, he got slowly up from his recliner and walked over to the chest. Henry bent down, picking the top from the floor, put the lid securely back into place. He still did not totally believe what happened, but he set the small box down carefully next to the television. Zeltman stood there for a moment unable to tear his eyes away until a satisfied smile of relief and happiness broke across his face.

"No, my dear," he said out loud, "trust me on this. I bought the box just for you."

The End

ITS A DARK RIDE

I SAW MYSELF dead, in a red room, motionless on the floor. Perhaps I had been deceased for some time; it was difficult to tell. The single light bulb in the room gave off a blood-colored hue, which prevented me from being able to tell the color of my skin.

I paused and looked around the red room; appearing to be a good size in dimensions—perhaps fifty feet by fifty feet. The room was decorated in an old Victorian style; there were oil portraits of people I didn't know on the walls. Each person appeared angry or sad in the paintings, that were framed with elaborate gilded wood. Beneath the largest picture was an old wooden writing table with a quill pen and a large stack of blank paper placed in the center of the table.

The room was without any natural light—there

were no windows—in the solid walls. What unnerved me was the fact that there was no door, and a sense of confinement flooded over me. I felt trapped in a sinister box, with no way of escape.

I walked over to where my body and knelt down cutting my hand when I placed it on the red carpet that appeared soft, but was hard and sharp—like a bed of a thousand needles. I let out a loud yelp quickly retracting my hand from the pain.

Leaning in to examine the body, I it cold to the touch like pressing my fingers on a marble surface. Most disturbing, was my face; it was distorted with my eyes to deteriorating, and my mouth hung open as if I had endured horrible pain.

I felt nauseated, I got back to my feet turning my attention elsewhere. The first thing I saw was a porcelain doll resting in a wicker chair made of dark wood large enough to seat two adults.

My eyes moved back to the porcelain doll, a female, covered in a blanket of red light. The toy had long blond hair and she was wearing a blue and white dress, reminiscent of the lead character from the old Alice in Wonderland stories, but the doll's face transformed before me.

The doll's face once that of a young blue-eyed girl, was now demonic. Her face had became elongated with blood-red eyes with her mouth opened wide in an evil grin exposing razor-sharp teeth. A second wave of panic came over me. I felt my knees give way in a wave of fear swept over me. The room became intensely hot, and objects in the room began to melt. As the exterior melted away, it left a hellish imprint. One of the pictures on the wall caught my eye – I watched in horror as the oil colors bled away and revealed a portrait of a monstrous demon that burned in flames.

As the temperature inside the red room increased, I saw my dead body sink into the floor, which now had become a small red sea of quicksand. I felt myself begin to slip into the tarry floor beneath me. Panicking, I tried to make a run for it , but the more I struggled, the deeper I sank into the floor. Within mere moments I was knee-deep in the burning red slush.

Even though the pain from liquefied floor was beyond anything I'd ever felt before, I refused to give up, even when my flesh stripped away from the bone with each step I took. I heard myself screaming in agony, still refusing to stop. I had no clue where I was headed but knew that it would be my end if I came to a complete stop.

By the time I reached the center of the room, the slush was up to my neck, and I froze in fear upon hearing a demonic laugh behind me. I was afraid, but forced myself to glance over my shoulder – it was the doll.

She still sat on the wicker chair that too sank into the unknown. Once the demon had nowhere else to stand, it also became engulfed in the red floor, bursting into flames once it made contact with the slush. All I could do was watch in horror as it sank, all the while, the creature never stopped its wicked laughter.

Turning my attention back to the room,. I got lost in the moment and had stopped moving. Before I could advance myself any further, I felt a pair of hands grab my feet; I was pulled underneath the red mush moments later.

#

I slowly opened my eyes and saw myself lying dead in a white room. I am motionless on the floor; perhaps I have been deceased for some time. I had been placed peacefully in the center of room that is quite large, and decorated in such a way reminiscent of a beach house. Large windows wrapped around the room displayed a beautiful view of a white, sandy beach and crystal blue ocean.

A gentle breeze drifted through the room filling the area with a pleasant smell of fresh seawater. A large white plush, bed at the far end rested neatly beneath another window making it appear as if I were looking at a beautiful painting capturing the lush green forest outside. *It was living art*, I thought to myself.

I sat on the edge of the bed looking around at the peaceful white room when I spotted a bowl of exotic fruit, a type I had ever seen before. I had to taste it, although I wasn't hungry. I picked up a piece, one that was on top, and bit into it. The flavor of tropical juice exploded in my mouth with the taste of nothing I had experienced before.

I finished the last bite, when I noticed a beautiful light oak desk resting beneath a window that faced east. On top of the desk, several hardbound books and a quill pen resting inside a jar of ink.

I walked over to the desk picking a book from the top of the stack. Opening it, I was welcomed by enchanting aroma of old paper,.but the book was empty. Returning the book to the top of the stack I made my way back to the bed. And crawling in, I found a comfortable spot directly in the center. It I felt I lying on clouds becoming fatigued. My body felt as if I had just finished a long journey, and it was now time to sleep, so I closed my eyes, and within moments, I was asleep.

#

Sometime later, I was awakened by someone who called my name. I leisurely sat up from the bed and was excited seeing my grandparents, along with other family members. Knowing I hadn't seen them for some time, I couldn't remember exactly why but that didn't matter.

As I got out of bed, grandmother told me everyone was gathered for a barbecue to celebrate my arrival. I followed everyone, realizing that my body was no longer in the center of the room. I was still uncertain why it had been there in the first place, deciding that it being gone, was for a better good.

I was greeted by my family members when I approached them, allowing them to lead led me outside. When I stopped at the doorway, they stopped as well and watched me run over to the desk and grabbed a book from the stack along with the jar of ink and the quill pen.

As I turned back and faced my family, they were huddled at the doorway. I held up the book and smiled. “For later,” I said.

The End

An Essay about Violence in our Society

Violence is everywhere in today's world, from video games to the six o'clock news, in the following text; we will look into the world of violence and what role it plays in our society.

Also, we will explore the theory that violence is simply a natural primal reaction due to overpopulation. In the end, we will hopefully have a deeper understanding of violence while asking, is violence an epidemic in our society, or is it merely a part of life as we know it?

There has been much talk about violence in our society of late, but why is it increasing? Did we have a surge in the births of sociopaths or people with Acute Personality Disorder, or is it the wrath of the Almighty in His divine plan to end the world? The answer will change depending on whom you ask. One of the biggest said causes of violence is claimed to result from the increasing violence that is added to today's video games. Certain people believe that as younger players witness horrific scenes of violence loaded with bloodshed, this will somehow warp our youth of today into serial killers of tomorrow.

Can we prove that allowing the Gamer the ability to create countless scenes filled with blood and death for hours at a time will warp the fragile minds of our poor innocent children? We have not been able to. Over the years, there have been countless studies that focus on the effects video games have on our society, with the scientific method employed innumerable times, and have resulted in findings all the same. The conclusion of one such study using a psychoanalytical approach stated that subjects with no history of psychosis remanded to have no signs of a new onset of psychosis after gaming. Researchers also found that whereas subjects that screened high in regards to having sociopathic behavior did show a slightly higher rate of interest in the parts that pertained to the blood and gore, in time did not show a substantial increase in overall psychosis.

So the fact be known, after several studies, the primary research shows that the myth of people being mentally affected by playing violent video games for an extended period and in effect causing people to develop violent behavior has been proven to be thus far fictional by the following esteemed universities: Stanford (Anderson & Bushman, 2001), Oxford (Gentile & Buckley, 2006), and Harvard (Funk &

Buchman, 2006).

Another theory that was made regarding why there is a growing level of violence in our society is the violence in media, particularly in movies. We can find violence in all forms, from the small screen to the big screen. These days all we have to do is turn on the television and thumb through a couple of channels before running into something that would fit in the definition of violence. One of the best examples of this is the newscasts. How often, then not, do we find the entire broadcast filled with death and gloom?

Newscasts are possibly the most visually disturbing avenue of media in the history of moving photography. Unlike movies or television shows, what is seen on the news is not fiction but is instead real life, and yet most people encourage others to watch at least one broadcast per day to keep up to date on current events.

But, movies on the silver screen get the worst rep when it comes to influential violence in our society. Since motion pictures are hands down the largest grossing medium in the way of media, it makes them an easy target for criticism. For decades film has been blamed for not only turning out blockbusters but sociopaths as well. A variety of groups from Parents Against Violence to a Southern Religious Organization have pointed their ever-blaming finger at movies as the sole cause of violent behavior in our world.

Yet, when we investigate these accusations with a scientific eye, no link could be found between psychosis and violent films. Much like with the findings with Video Games, subjects that showed higher signs of sociopathic behavior and the ones that did not show any abnormal signs whatsoever ultimately resulted in the same.

The theory states that after being exposed to such levels of violence, the subjects should develop some noticeable behavior change, so what do the findings conclude? The final decision is that after several hours spent watching high levels of violent films, neither group demonstrated an indication of a possible urge for violence. The theory that motion pictures directly affect society's violent behavior is a myth that it is and has no scientific connection whatsoever.

Yet another explanation for the growing level of violence in our society is the one of spiritual belief. Many followers of a higher power believe that this is a direct effect of their God, as He has begun His holy wrath on the world for living years in sin. The majority of the Christian faith believes in an apocalyptic ending to the world, where the final good and evil will collide in a war to end all wars. Many of these religions look forward to the end, as it will be proof of the authenticity of their faith.

For centuries the increase in violence has been theorized as proof that the "End Times are coming." In these mainly Christian beliefs, life for all humans must become intolerable by way of the last World War with violence never before seen. But, if we put this theory into a scientific view, there is no significant evidence whatsoever supporting this theory, even though many people interject the Bible as a historical source for their faith.

The Bible itself is not historically valid. It is a book that was initially created and written by several people who claimed to be followers of Christ in 49 A.D. in the Hebrew language. And was originally commissioned to be assembled as one whole book (instead of several small ones) by Roman Emperor Caesar Constantine, a Pagan Sun Worshiper, in 331 A.D. (William L. Langer ENCYCLOPEDIA OF WORLD HISTORY, Pages 97 - 100).

Nowadays, the Bible read here in the United States has been rewritten and translated multiple times before ending in our modern translation. For example, it was originally written in Hebrew, then translated into Greek/Roman, followed by a conversion to Latin, then into Ole English, and finally made into Modern English. It has been said by many scholars that there was a high possibility that the original intended context may have been lost from the various revisions. Yet, millions of people follow the text with no questions or thoughts about its possible authenticity.

So the theory that a divine hand of an Almighty Creator is the source for the growing level of violence in today's society has also been added to the myth section and the previous theories mentioned. Though this theory may be the biggest among the people, it is the least when it comes to a historical or scientific angle.

The next theory to the cause of the growing levels of violence in our society is caused by a person's exposure to their environment. It has been hypothesized for many years that because someone has been raised or lived in a hostile environment, it will ultimately cause the said person to develop a violent psychosis and then turn into a homicidal sociopath. The argument of whether the environment affects a person has been debated for several years by many scholars.

Let's take a look at an example of the environment of a person. If you have a young man raised in the ghetto of South Central Los Angeles, will they turn out to be a thug involved in drugs and street gangs?

Though scientific data points to the possibility and is definitely on the high side, it is not a sure fact that the young man will indeed turn out to a drug-addicted street thug. Yes, the environment does play a large role in a person's behavior, but does it affect how they will end up in life? Can the area in which you live automatically predestine your outcome?

Can the man who was raised in South Central Los Angeles become something of greater importance to society? Absolutely. It is solely up to the person to what they want to do with their life. It is up to them if they're going to be a lowlife street thug or a high-paid lawyer. As of the many creatures in this world, we are the gifted ones who have something called free will. A person can become anything that they want to become if they want it bad enough.

Nothing is predestined for us, and we make life what we make it. So, therefore, the theory that a person's environment has a direct effect on our violent society has not been proven true. Though it may have some persuasion on the person themselves, it is ultimately up to that person in what role they will take in society, whether it is a positive one or negative, it is their decision.

It has been clinically proven that a man who grows up in the Ritz of Beverly Hills, who lived a rich life and went to the best schools, has the same chance of turning out to be a homicidal sociopath. It is the decision of the individual in the path they wish to take, but the reason as to why comes with a biological answer.

These people are born with mental disorders; it has been discovered that genetics play a key role in sociopaths in one way or another. It is the inability of said people to remorse for their violent crimes. In essence, these people are born without consciousness. Therefore, they don't comprehend that these acts on an emotional level, which makes them so dangerous.

But, this essay is about the main reason why there is so much violence in our society. With sociopaths totaling less than one percent of the world's population, we cannot state that this was the leading factor in why violence levels are so high. It may contribute to it on a small level, but this is not the sole cause of our problem.

The answer to our question may go back to 1971 on the campus of Michigan State University. Researchers wanted to understand why violence occurs more in overpopulated areas (such as New York, Los Angeles, and Chicago) rather than in less rural areas. But in the end, their findings gave a better explanation of why violence in our society is escalating, more than anything else.

The Researcher sat up an experiment using an empty hundred-gallon aquarium and several dozen laboratory rats. They placed a lab rat into the large aquarium every five minutes and then evaluated their reactions once they were inside the confines. In the beginning, the rodents appeared to be comfortable with their new environment. As more were added, the creatures appeared to interact with each other, but once the tank's area became full, the rats seemed to segregate into their little corners.

Once, the aquarium's entire surface was covered with the body of a rat, and the animals refused to move. They stayed in their spot and kept to themselves. The researchers noted an interesting finding. Once the entire tank's entire area became full, and the researchers continued to place a rat inside, the rats moved apart to create an open space for the newcomer. The animals did this consistently until there was no possible room left, so what happens once there is no more room?

The rats themselves became erratically hostile. They turned violent and eventually killed each other until the population returned to a small size, and then rodents returned to their original behavior. The test was repeated several times, and with each attempt, the result came out the same. They all turned on each other until their numbers dropped.

The researchers concluded that it was a primal survival instinct, which caused the upheaval once the aquarium became too full. Those creatures may not have understood that once the area became too populated, it became uninhabitable. Therefore lowers their chance of survival, but out of pure instinct, to react in a manner that would eventually bring their chances of survival back to a safer rate.

With these findings, researchers applied this to the current problem as a species with high levels of violence and concluded the following . . .

The researchers believe that the growing amount of violence in our society is the direct result of our primal instinct for survival due to the overpopulation of the planet. As a whole, we are overpopulated by one-third of the world's population. This is thought to be the general cause of our violence, but the researchers also explained that this was why large cities, such as Los Angeles and New York, have so much more crime and violence than the lesser populated areas.

In the end, violence is only a primal reaction to the ever-growing population of our planet. If so, then does that mean that there is no escaping the flow of violence, which will only escalate as the number of people in our world continues to grow? The facts point to only one concrete answer to these questions.

The answer is simply no. There appears to be no escape from the hold that violence has on our society as long as our population continues to grow at an unprecedented rate. As much as we would like to think otherwise, the reality is that though we try to civilize our world, the pure primal instinct of survival is more significant than any other solution we can come up with.

Works Cited

Anderson & Bushman. (2001) http://www.apa.org/science/psa/sb-anderson.html

Funk & Buchman. (2006) *Journal of Communication* Volume 46 Issue 2, Pages 19 - 32 Published: 7 Feb 2006

Gentile & Buckley. (2006) *Violent Video Game Effects on Children and Adolescents*

Theory, Research. and Public Policy Published: January 2007

William L. Langer ENCYCLOPEDIA OF WORLD HISTORY, Pages 97 - 100 Published: September 1901

TAKE ME HOME

I am finished—unable to continue the fight,
May the Reaper come take my soul tonight.
Lately it has become hell to keep me whole,
The lifelong war has finally taken its toll.
Never will I win, forever to be poor;
I do not want to be here anymore!
So can you please just take me home?
Free me from this, so I may roam.
In time you won't remember me, but that is fine;
Alone I will be, though my soul will remain mine.
Everyone that I have known has already walked out the door,
Reaffirming that I don't want to be here anymore!
I don't want a blessing read from a tome,
So, please, if you would just take me home!

Farewell!

Slowly they moved toward the grave; the site was dark and dead, uncared for, for countless decades. Once they were a few yards away, Christine noticed the graffiti, written in red chalk, that read: Forgotten.

"Heathens," Christine mumbled under her breath. "Why would someone want to vandalize the old grave of a sweet boy? Will you take me over to the grave marker? I want to try and clean that crap off."

"Of course," the young orderly replied and began to push the wheelchair closer to the headstone.

As they moved onto the soil that held her lover's remains, Christine felt a shift in the ground; it was wet and sludgy. Her wheelchair's tires sank into the mud, becoming immobile from that point. Unnerved, the old woman turned and asked with a slight smile, "Help me onto the ground, dear."

The young orderly's mouth dropped open. "But, Miss Lincoln, you'll get wet and dirty."

Christine nodded. "I know, but I can't leave Eddy's grave like this."

The young orderly lifted Christine from her wheelchair and lowered her slowly down next to the headstone. Once she was secure on the unkept ground, she quickly proceeded to remove the red chalk with the palm of her frail hand. But, to her dismay, it only smudged the letters across the stone, which made the marker even less attractive.

Christine looked down at her hand and sighed. "I'm sorry, Eddy. I tried to help."

A silence followed her words as she sat next to the vandalized headstone, her eyes fixed on her hand covered with red chalk. Christine's thought traveled back to that night, and saw Eddy lying in a pool of blood as he died. His hands appeared dirty and bloody. Tiny puddles of blood collected in his nail beds.

Christine returned to reality noticing someone pulling on her wrist. As she came to, she quickly realized that the young orderly was screaming uncontrollably and soon bellowed out in horror when she noticed a bloody hand coming up from the ground grabbing her wrist.

A second hand erupted from the dead Earth and clutched her other wrist tightly, Christine pulled frantically, but she was in a vice.

Eddy's longing vice.

The young orderly frantically screamed while she watched on in horror as the hands slowly pulled Christine into the grave to be rejoined with her one true love.

THE END

They both gasped when the two women saw a single loose telephone wire draped over the tree and led straight into the ground exactly where Edward's remains rested.

THE END

ABOUT THE AUTHOR

David K. Montoya was first published in 1992 with the release of an independent comic book entitled, *M-Team*. In a span of ten years, he wrote over two hundred stories for that genre. At the turn of the millennia, went to work as a Producer on a small horror film and co-wrote the script for Body Bag. The following year went back into comics with the release of a one-shot named, *SmasH*. In 2003, fell in love with traditional literature and begin writing short stories. From then until now, he has written eighty-two stories. Like the multi-award winning series *THE END* and his Children's Book, *The Missing Unicorn in the Land of the Zombie Fairies*.

Montoya has been published in a wide variety of publications *The World of Myth: Anthology Volumes I, II, III and IV, Weird Mask Magazine, The World of Myth Magazine, Zombie EPICdemic Anthology, Getting Short Stories Published: A Guidebook, Unwelcomed: Stories of Hauntings and Possessions, Monster Within: Tales of a Tortured Mind* and his own anthology of dark stories titled as an ode to his mentor's book, *It's A Dark Ride*. In 2023 found him publishing his murder mystery epic novel, *Through the Eyes of Madness* and his chapbook, *ALIS: A Science Fiction Love Story*.

That is only the writing side of him, as he prefers to stay private. He lives in Southern California with his three children, dog, and his annoying ass cat.

www.ingramcontent.com/pod-product-compliance
Lightning Source LLC
LaVergne TN
LVHW090520110826
845146LV00003B/931

* 9 7 9 8 9 9 0 6 0 8 3 2 0 *